Samiyah

L.R. Hicks

LeeLoo Publishing / Texas

LeeLoo Publishing™
http://leeloopub.com/

First Print Edition

ISBN-10: 0-9988843-1-6
ISBN-13: 978-0-9988843-1-8

Acknowledgements

Lady Vi and Wuffle Puff. You know who you are my darlings.

Ghost of a Chance by Rush

1. Samiyah

I am Samiyah.

I am beautiful. I know this. In my childhood this beauty was advantageous. Now it is the very thing keeping me locked up in this place. This revolving door of leering buyers and wishful thinkers. The ranch.

My black hair, thick and shiny, cascades past my small waist accentuating ample breasts and wide hips. Long legs with shapely thighs covered in dark caramel colored skin usually bring attention to me first. Then it is always my eyes that keep it. Emerald and shining out from a perfect symmetrical face of long dark lashes, high cheekbones, and full lips.

The slaver who bought me from my parents, Lady Cademe, is both my jailor and my savior. She purchased me nine years ago for a ridiculous sum of money hoping to make fifteen times what she paid. She will make more than that. Her staff grooms me in every way possible. Walking. Diet. Exercise and eloquent speech therapy. Music and dance lessons. I am proficient in all these things. Aliens love me especially. I am their ideal of a human woman, but I am the same for my own kind. Ideal.

But with each bid, the duration of my stay in the safe bubble of my lady's ranch extends. It is the law. Weekly I have a new bidder. And weekly I think my jailor realizes I may be more a curse than a blessing to her business. But perhaps not. My presence alone drives up the sale of her other stock. Rumor of my beauty attracts the buyers, but when they realize they cannot afford me they purchase another stock. I remain in this perpetual bidding war. It is my lady's punishment for following Galactic Cluster Law I suppose.

I don't mind it here. I am untouched, safe. I enjoy the company of my fellow stock, other prisoners, and an old parishioner. We all call him Parishioner, at his insistence. It is the only name he wants us to know. He is the best company. From what he says, he came to the ranch trying to convince my lady to rescind her life of sin. To let us all go. To free not only her stock, but herself from eternal damnation. But my lady is of Gnolian blood. Humanoids with grey skin, blonde hair, and silver eyes. We all know Gnolians live for eons. She is young for her species and has plenty of time for her sins.

And so now Parishioner, finding himself unable to leave until he has freed us, keeps jolly company and comforts those who are not so lucky as I. Those my lady plucks out of our modest cabins and thrusts into a world of sexual servitude. This is the fate that awaits me. Someday.

The old man, stooping, overweight, with kindness behind his blue eyes, sits on the edge of my bed regaling me with a story of his youth when my lady comes to me herself, for I am her most prized possession, and opens the door to my small cabin. A new buyer is here to have a look at me. I rise with the smooth grace I was taught and smile at her. I do not let it waver as I notice the twinkle in her eye and smile on her face. She thinks this one is serious. My stomach turns beneath my flawless midriff. The silk and satin covering only the necessities, fabric hanging between my legs and over my breasts, swish as I glide after her into the desert sun of our ship.

Our ship. My home. The ranch is an Atmo-ship. Very expensive. The best way to travel through deep space. Instead of living in a long metal tube like most ships, we live on a patch of real land with an atmospheric bubble encasing us. There is real wind and clouds and a blue sky above. A miniature nuclear reaction circles us in a day and night cycle like our very own sun. It is as close to living on home planet as I can get, even though I personally have never been. Our lady specializes in human stock and keeps us as happy and healthy as she can—another reason she allows Parishioner to remain at her expense. He helps to counsel those who would otherwise be difficult, unwittingly doing more harm than good.

My lady only sells to those aliens and humans who breathe our same atmosphere. Like she does. No masks or helmets allowed. She guarantees her stock and won't have any of us stifled after so much nurturing and care. Her reputation is at stake. We have a lifetime warranty. Only void if our master murders us. We can also be returned for a discount price once we reach old age. In my time here, I have seen a handful of old stock return.

Sand blows around in small whirlwinds in the distance. Why she chooses the desolate desert over green forests and fields the parishioner tells me about, I don't know. I theorize it may be to do with our lady's own preference. The desert befits her most, and other than myself, I suppose she is the one who must live here longest.

My potential buyer waits under a tent, hidden beneath white robes and a cowl, sitting on a wicker chair I witness many romps grace. Two of my fellow stock fan him and his associates standing around. Another holds a tray of sweating cold drinks. I glide towards him. My eyes lock with his. Instead of being lost in my gaze, however, he scowls. Annoyance. He sneers and stands, pointing at me.

"She dares look me in the eye?"

This doesn't faze my lady and her smile remains, "Samiyah, look down."

I do as she commands and stare down at my manicured toes. I possess soft hands and feet, having never worked hard labor in my life.

The buyer grunts, and at the top of my vision crosses his arms.

"Come," my lady gestures to the lounge cabin where I can be put on proper display. Many times a day I follow her in and do my tricks, but already I feel this time is different.

The buyer trails her with his companions and I know to wait as they enter the open archway of the white adobe structure. Red curtains lined with gold threading billow in the breeze. They disappear down the long hallway I know lies beyond, into the cool darkness of the lounge. A relief from the desert heat. At this moment I know my lady guides them with a handheld light to sit on the plush and vibrant pillows of the lounge. Other stock, some praying they don't catch a buyer's eye, give them drinks and treats. After the buyer and his entourage settle, each in their place around a small stage, my lady will cast the room into darkness with the death of her light.

Samiyah

I play this ritual in my head so I have perfect timing. I know the lights around the small stage wait for me, igniting in small flames. Creating mood, as my lady puts it. The decorum carefully selected for their gilded appearance twinkle in the moving light. Shadows dance before I begin mine.

Taking a deep breath, I glide past the billowing curtains into darkness. The path is in my memory as I navigate the hallway. Another stock opens the heavy quiet door to the lounge and I enter in silence. Six pairs of glowing eyes follow me in the darkness around the small circular stage. With practice I step up into its light and twirl. The silk hanging between my legs lifts up with the movement, giving them a peek at my pure genitals. This is what buyers truly prize. I am never to show them all, as per my lady's command. Only my owner will have that privilege.

I know my lady, watching from the darkness, nods with approval as I lift the delicate fabric covering my breasts up to the edge of my nipple. A tease of rose colored skin. I still my twirl and settle my clothes into their proper place. Then, hidden as well, other stock play music for me to dance to.

It is the same choreography I have danced a thousand times. More than that. And the memory of its movement dominates my body, allowing me time to wonder about this buyer. Some of them are hostile such as him, some are sweet and nurturing. Hoping to lure me. Many a number ask me to run away with them when alone. My stomach turns as do my hips with the rhythm of the music. I will have alone time with this buyer soon. My least favorite part of the process. It is always uncomfortable. The music lulls to a stop and my voice lilts into an echo around the enclosed space. My singing is as perfect as my body. Afterward, normally there is clapping, but not today.

My lady kills the false fire of stage lights and the room illuminates in a soft glow. Remembering the buyer's hostile nature, I lower my eyes before they can meet his. I don't want to look at him anyway. Now is alone time.

My lady puts herself between us, breaking his stare. He huffs.

Her voice is firm. She takes orders from no one, "Now, you may have a moment alone with her. There is only one rule: do not touch her. I will be watching."

She gestures to the metal door, which is now open, letting sunlight spill into the lounge, breaking the spell of fabrics and accessories of a culture long dead from home planet. My lady spent a lot of time and money putting this room together to set a mood for the process. I like it. I wish I could decorate my cabin like this.

The buyer ticks his head to the door and his companions stand. They file out. My lady follows and shuts the door after herself. Now there is darkness and dim light. The buyer stands. He is close now and I stare up at him. His pink eyes narrow and I can get a clear look.

His light eyes are offset by a dark blue tinge to his smooth scaly skin. He isn't entirely human, but some. Enough. Enough for complete copulation with me. The thought of that possibility makes butterflies in my stomach dance again. He pulls back the white cloth of his cowl that protects him from the sun from his forehead, and thick black hair, not too different from mine, falls in a braid over his shoulder. He is handsome but for the hatred pouring out of his stare. And yet, he is familiar. Have I seen him before? Maybe he is a disgruntled buyer from the past.

"I didn't say you can look up."

I find my voice, "And?"

"Defiant," he sneers.

"Yes," I don't blink. I know him from somewhere. "You are not my master."

He smiles with sharp teeth.

"I will be."

His confidence shakes mine, but I have danced this dance before. I know the moves and they never end the way the buyer thinks it will.

"Sit down," he orders.

I do no such thing, taking pleasure in crossing my arms.

"I said sit down," he raises his voice, hoping to scare me.

I cannot tell him how many times I have been coddled, cooed, and yelled at. I don't budge.

He steps up to my stage and hovers his hands over my curves. I know the hunger in his eyes. I have seen that too. Too many times to count. He is not special, despite what he wishes.

He paces the room, screaming, yelling in his native tongue. I don't understand it, and I don't care. I study the room I have graced a thousand times. Everything in its place. Nothing out of order. I do not understand this familiar buyer's anger, but it is not my business either. He will be like all the others. He will put in his bid and I will only see him on the occasion he comes back to decide if he wants to bid again. But they do not all come back, most give their highest offer.

He snarls, whipping my attention back to him. I am bored with him already. The butterflies in my stomach nap as he approaches.

His hands stop short of my arms. He does as he likes, but not now. My lady is not one to trifle with. Her reputation precedes her as does mine. He will not touch me. This makes me smile, which infuriates him further.

"Fak!" He throws the cowl back over his head and storms out.

"Goodbye," as I watch him recede. I imagined a difficult alone time. He was not the worst.

I step down from the stage and lay on the soft pillows while I wait.

Moments later my lady returns with her tablet. The unnatural glow lights up her smile. It is rare she grins, but it tells me he made a sizable offer for me. I swallow my concern.

"Come, Samiyah."

I nod and follow her to my cabin at the edge of the cluster of small homes we, the stock, occupy. Parishioner waits for me there, as he always does, and he stands with a smile. He takes my hand and pats it.

"Are you all right?" he asks.

I smile and nod, "Always." I squeeze his hand in return and face my lady.

She holds up her tablet and turns it round to me.

I cannot breathe. This number cannot be right. I swallow again and curl my perfect arms around my small waist. Parishioner puts his arm around my shoulders, making my lady frown, and keeps me from collapsing.

"My Lord," he whispers. "Six million?"

My lady nods, the smile returns as she turns the tablet back to herself for confirmation of her happiness.

"Yes. I think we finally have a buyer."

I lick my lips and will saliva into my dry mouth, "This cannot be."

"This is sixty times what I paid for you." She rests her hand on my warm cheek, "You have done well. I think you were worth the wait."

I nod in automatic compliance. She leaves my one room cabin and shuts the metal door behind herself.

Parishioner sits with me on my plush bed and my eyes wander the sparse contents. The carpet is thick and brown. No windows, but a skylight in the ceiling. I used to have windows until someone tried to steal me in the night. Gnolian metal reinforces my cabin. I cannot escape. They cannot take me. The door auto-locks when my lady lies down for the night. Over the adobe walls I have pictures of home planet that Parishioner and potential buyers give me. I long for green forests and running water. In a dresser I have sleeping clothes, lounge wear, and changes of costume. I have to perform often, not just for buyers, but onlookers who pay only to see me as well as guests of my lady. In the bedside are trinkets my lady lets me keep from childhood. Nothing of importance, only empty memories.

Tears well in my eyes.

Parishioner sighs and hugs me close to him. I love him. My old man. I lay my head on his drooping shoulder and cry. At first slow, hot tears. And now heaves. Sobs. I have not cried like this since I came to the ranch. I cover my face with my hands and for the first time in my life I feel ugly.

"I cannot..." I can't breathe. The thought.

"Perhaps...perhaps someone will outbid him," Parishioner offers.

I shake my head.

The highest bid I have to date is 2.4 million speks. No one will come close to six. Less likely to surpass it.

"What was he like?" he asks.

I blink and wipe my wet cheeks. I stare at the glassy surface of my fingers. "Mean."

He nods. "Not someone you want to spend your life with."

"No," I shake my head.

He inhales a shuddering breath and frowns. I know this face. He thinks. I straighten, forcing his arm off my shoulders, I am so much taller than he, and take his hand in mine.

"There is nothing to be done," I say. "My lady will not allow it. If she is happy with this it will be done. You know this."

"I do," his voice wavers. "I do."

I have known some of my buyers for years. Most of my life here. Each time they are outbid they return, I remind them of what I offer as the jewel of the ranch, and they outbid the previous buyer with the smallest sum they can. But this time, only a handful return. Only a few can afford this price. And even less can afford it without emptying their entire coffer. And I know they question if I am worth that. Worth losing everything else they own.

It seems I am not.

The bid remains. It has twenty-four cycles before closing. It has never surpassed seven. Until today.

The sun turns up. Hot. Wind blows harder and sand swirls everywhere. My lady must be feeling unwell for her to do this to us. It is inhospitable, but I cannot complain. My cabin is cool and the sand cannot penetrate the seals on my door and skylight, but I am busier than ever, despite the bid staying where it is. More people, buyers and curious onlookers, want to see me. They know this is their last chance before I am privately owned.

Parishioner is quiet, but not distant. He spends as much time with me as he can while my lady spends as little. I think she will miss me. Just a little.

My lady keeps her dock open during business hours and it is full. Crowds are everywhere to gawk at me. I hardly spend time in my cabin. I have to walk, dance, sing, and simply exist in their presence until I can no more. I tire and know I will be more so once sold.

I accept my fate with anxiety. I do not know what the buyer, my soon to be owner, Varashka is his name, will want with me. I have an idea of course, but it is not a pleasant one. For me, at least.

The dock closes and our sun suspends at the edge of our ship in eternal sunset. My lady sometimes leaves it like this, just for me. I like the orange illumination, but am usually too busy during the day to enjoy it. Sometimes she lets me have extra, like today. Her guilt bathes me in its light.

A single figure emerges from the dock after-hours and I furrow my dark brows. I am in my free time and sit on the small porch of my cabin with Parishioner. In waves of heat the figure is dressed in black, and has long legs. Probably tall. I catch my breath as he grows close. He comes toward me. I search for any sign of my lady. It is rare for her to not be out here with a buyer. He must be a buyer. As he draws near I hope he is. His skin is paper white and eyes large and black. He isn't entirely human, but enough. Just enough. He is handsome and I have never felt an immediate attraction like this. His black clothes are leather, common in space travel to combat the cold. He carries a helmet, telling me he did not go through the customer entrance to our ship, but the service gate. Buyers always have their extra items checked by security. His gait is confident. A gun hangs low at his hip. This surprises me as well, no weapons are ever allowed on board. His dark hair is a chocolate color and unkempt, long and thick in the breeze. I wish to card my fingers through it.

I sit up in my wicker chair, self conscious, for perhaps the first time in my life, in my lounge wear. I'm not in silks and jewels, but a cotton tunic and breeches. My hair is braided back from my angular face. Parishioner doesn't notice the man and keeps his focus on the book of his people, reading. I watch the man, but he doesn't watch me. His dark eyes rest on Parishioner. I tap my friend on the shoulder and he grunts, marking his place with a ribbon bound to the binding of the book, and closes it. He removes his glasses and smiles at me.

"Yes my dear?"

I point to the stranger.

He follows my gaze and his grey brows rise. He laughs, surprising me, and drops the book he finds most precious on the porch by his feet. He lifts from the chair and the young man drops his helmet, opening his arms. I watch them embrace, clapping each other on the back. The stranger stands heads taller than my old man and ruffles his hair, earning a look of reprisal from him. This must be why the man came through the service entrance. He isn't here to see me.

I stand up, but remain on my porch. I am so accustomed to being noticed, I enjoy this moment. Observing without reciprocation. I cannot help but smile seeing my old man so happy. He elates.

They speak softly and the breeze muffles their speech. I wring my hands. I hope this man hasn't come to take my friend when I need him most. The stranger gestures to my cabin, but Parishioner corrects him, pointing to his own. I am forgotten as they walk away. The stranger doesn't glance back.

Now it is cycle eighteen. Too close to twenty-four. My acceptance of fate reverses with each hour another bid doesn't come. I have trouble sleeping. I have no appetite. And I am only thankful to the god my Parishioner worships that he is still here. He does not tell me who the stranger is, or what he wants. I do not ask. Though I want to know, I respect his privacy as he always does mine.

My buyer returns, much to my lady's pleasure and dismay. Her smile falters now when speaking of my price and departure. She cannot look at me with pride as she once did. I think she regrets, but it is too late. The pair cramp into my cabin as my future owner glances over my few possessions. Now in his presence my pride escapes me and I do as he asks. Sitting when he wants and keeping my eyes downward. My lady allows him to caress my cheek and run his hands down my arms. Another sign my fate is sealed. I can feel his tension, the raw strength he holds back from me. I swallow my fear and keep from swaying. I want to fall against the bed. My feet itch to run. Instead I am still and quiet.

"I think we can agree no one will outbid me," he says.

My lady frowns and tightens her grip on the tablet, "I think it is safe to say. Not impossible, but improbable."

"Then you will respect my wishes?" his baritone echoes in my cabin.

She nods.

"I don't want anymore onlookers. She is mine," he spares her a glance. "Mine. All that's left is formality."

My lady nods again, "As you wish."

He runs his fingers through my hair. A surprisingly gentle caress. He keeps hold of the end and smells, inhaling deep. He fists my locks before releasing them.

"I hope you enjoy your retirement," he mutters, leaving.

She follows him outside with no reply. My door shuts.

I gasp a shuddering breath and sit on my bed. I hug myself. Sweat drips down my temples. In my metal door is a small hole through which I can see any who approach. I stand and lean my hot body against the cool surface and watch as they disappear from view into her office. Most likely for paperwork. There is a crowd again today expecting me to entertain, but I cannot wait. I slip on my loungewear and leave the cabin. The visitors must always stay a certain distance from my cabin, and so I walk around behind it, shielding myself from their prying eyes with my home and others in the cluster. I know this path well and open the door into Parishioner's cabin. I slip inside the two room building and lock the door behind myself. I lean my forehead on it a moment before turning to find a surprise waiting in his front parlor.

The stranger sits in Parishioner's chair with a mug of cold water held up to his lips. His dark eyes watch me over the rim. I blush under his unblinking gaze. The seat across from him is empty.

Samiyah

I open my mouth and suck in a breath, but keep my question at the edge of my tongue. I close my lips and breathe outward.

The stranger lowers his mug, resting his forearm on his knee, leaning forward.

"You must be Samiyah," he says.

I swallow and nod.

"He's gone to get something from your master's storage. He'll be right back."

I nod again and purse my lips.

He gestures to the other chair, "Sit."

I shake my head, unlock the door, and step away from it. He makes me uncomfortable. I don't know why. It isn't bad, like with Varashka, but it isn't good. He keeps his dark eyes on mine, never wavering to the rest of me like most. He leans back in the chair, resting the cool mug on his thigh.

The door opens beside me and Parishioner steps through. He turns to me and smiles. I return it.

"Do you mind?" he asks, juggling scrolls in his arms.

I take them without hesitation and follow him to the back of the cabin where his bed, kitchenette, and study are. The stranger stands and trails behind, his booted feet heavy on the wood planks beneath us. He stands just behind me and a shiver runs up my spine. I'm aware of his eyes studying us as we lay the scrolls on Parishioner's messy desk. I think it is a dark wood beneath, but it is rare he has it uncovered.

"I think these will serve your needs," Parishioner says.

"You know my needs," the stranger answers.

Parishioner sighs, "Taren, I can't—"

"Sylvester."

"No."

They begin to argue.

"Sylvester?" I ask.

This stops them.

I smile, "This is your name, Parishioner?"

He glares at Taren, the stranger.

"I think you need to leave."

"C'mon," the stranger comes to me and, almost touching, lays his hands on the desk.

I back away from him, towards my old man.

"You're making her uncomfortable. You need to go. I can't help you. I'm not a young man anymore."

Taren laughs, "You've never been young so long as I've known you. And I'm not making her anything."

The young man glances at me, his eyes twinkling.

"I gave you my answer," Parishioner says.

"I can't do this without you."

"I said I can't leave!" Parishioner's hands shake. His cheeks flush. I do not see him like this often.

I rest my hand on his shoulder and he shudders a deep breath.

"I can't leave them," he whispers. "I can't leave her. Not now. Not like this."

Taren turns on me, "So *she's* why you won't come?"

He grabs my hand and I gasp. Parishioner snatches the stranger's wrist and flicks it, forcing him to release me.

"You can't touch her."

"What?" Taren's dark brows furrow. "Why?" He cocks his head to the side, "Is she sick?"

"You know why."

"We can take her with us." Taren shrugs. Like it is nothing.

My laugh starts soft and low, in my gut, and works its way up and out. I cover my face with my hands. Tears slide down my cheeks, not with joy, but with a wish. A wish it is that simple. To just leave.

"I..." the man in black frowns.

Parishioner shakes his head and puts his arm around my shuddering shoulder.

"Hypocrite," Taren mutters. "Can't be touched my ass."

"I'll make you a deal," my old man begins.

The young man raises his brows, "I'm listening."

"I'll come with you, if we can take her with us."

"I just offered—"

Parishioner waves his hand, silencing his friend. "I think you need to understand just what I'm asking of you."

Taren nods slowly.

The old man swallows and turns me round to face him. I wipe my wet cheeks.

"Samiyah, my child," he takes a shuddering breath. "If I can get you out of here, will you come with me?"

I open my mouth and close it. This is not the first time I have been asked this, but it is different. This is my old man. For the first and only time it tempts me. I don't want to leave, but I will no matter what. Whether with my old man or new owner. I will leave.

"I will be safe?" I ask, a whisper. I don't want to be heard. My lady sees everything. Hears everything. I made the mistake of displeasing her only once.

Parishioner nods, "He can keep you safe."

I glance to the man in black, the stranger. Taren. He seems capable, but so have many others.

"Will he...touch me?" I ask. Confusion crosses the stranger's face, but Parishioner knows my meaning.

"No, he will not touch you."

"Unless you want me to," the man laughs to himself.

I frown.

"He's joking," my old man glares at his young counterpart. "He doesn't mean it. He's trying to make me angry."

Taren clears his throat and presents a somber expression. He waves his hands in a crossing motion.

"Will not touch."

I like him, but don't trust him.

I shake my head, "No."

I back away from Parishioner, towards the door. I shake my head again, "I can't." I don't want to cry again. Why do I cry so much now?

"I'm sorry," I say as I run out.

I expect my Parishioner to leave any cycle now, but he does not. He stays and attends to me, and the other stock, when he can. With crowds to see me leave, my lady sells most of the stock left and I notice new ones do not replace them. She no longer buys and now I understand Varashka's well wishing of her retirement. My lady is done with us, this place. This business. Perhaps she waits on me to be done. Perhaps she always did.

The stranger, Taren, remains here. Begging. Pleading with my Parishioner. He doesn't talk to or look at me when I am near. He waits for my Parishioner to return home before he speaks with him. As time grows short, he only stays in Parishioner's cabin. Helping my old man pack his own things. I think he may be angry with me, and I don't like it. I don't know why.

My home fades. Even if I escape, there will be nothing to come back to.

Samiyah

It is time.

My drawers are empty. I leave a small silk case of my few possessions on the front porch of my cabin. There is no one here anymore. A ghost town. The stock are gone, except those who remain to serve only my lady. She is here, waiting for me with her tablet. Her eyes are cold. Her smile fake. She is both sad and glad to see me go. No visitors are here to watch. I swallow, all of my training surfaces as I struggle to stay still. My new owner, now truly my master, comes for me. He is excited with a light step. He smiles, his sharp teeth gleaming in the sunlight. His eyes rake over my curves hidden beneath the black spacesuit he had tailored for me to wear on this journey. My hair, carefully pinned up, exposes my neck and shoulders to the hot wind. I feel naked.

My lady stops him short of me, just outside the shade of my porch.

"The money transfer must finish before she is yours."

Varashka nods and clasps his hands.

"And," my lady begins softly. "You will allow her to say her goodbyes."

My new master scowls, but knows he must obey. My lady will not transfer my papers until she wishes.

I bite the inside of my lip. Parishioner emerges from his cabin, his own cases packed and ready. His friend, Taren, begins hauling them to the service docks.

I watch my lady, who never takes her eyes from my new master, "May I?"

"You may," she stares her tablet.

I hesitate, take a step, turn and bow, and dismiss myself from my new master. He smirks and crosses his arms. His excitement frightens me. I walk, with purpose, to my old man. His smile doesn't reach his blue eyes, but he holds his arms open for me. I walk into them and close my own around him. My chin rests on his head of grey hair and I close my eyes. He is careful, as always, not to hug me too tightly, but I want to squeeze him. I don't want to let him go. Panic rises with my heartbeat. After this, I will go where my angry owner wishes me.

"Are you all right?" he asks.

I shake my head. "No. I'm not."

He pulls away. His brows furrow.

"Samiyah," my lady calls over the wind.

I need to go, but I don't. I grip his arms. My eyes widen.

"I'm scared," I whisper.

Parishioner frowns, "I'm sorry."

"Samiyah," my lady's voice rises.

I do not go. "I change my mind." My breaths come short. I can't breathe, "I change my mind. Help me. Please."

Parishioner glances over my shoulder to those who wait for me.

"Samiyah!" my lady snaps her fingers and points down to the sandy ground next to her.

I purse my lips and wipe the fear from my face. I must go. I release the old man as he lets go of me.

He's speechless, I know. I can feel what he wants to say. His regrets. His fears, and hopes, for me.

I saunter back towards my new master. The transfer is complete.

"No copulation on my property. Leave." My lady smiles at me, empty, and turns away. She returns to her home, not looking back once.

Samiyah

In the warm breeze, I bend to retrieve my case, but my master stills me. Now that he has me, now that I am his to command, he is patient.

He flicks his hand and one of his followers, hidden in white robes, picks up my case. Another steps forward and fastens a delicate silver chain to my wrist, the end of which is held in my master's hand. He turns, and I follow, keeping slack in the chain as I know I should. I can't remember what is beyond the atmosphere of the ship, but darkness looms ahead as it thins. Stars twinkle on the horizon as the false sun of home sets and remains behind us. My lady leaves it there, just for me. One last time. Metal and humming electricity line a gate separating us from the dock and beyond that is the vacuum of space.

A companion of my master, a human with delicate hands, fastens a helmet and gloves that lock into place along the metal bands of my spacesuit, ensuring the seal. Oxygen pumps into my helmet and I blink in the momentary breeze. I glance back over my shoulder, to my special sunset, before the gate unlocks and silent stillness greets us. The sunset fades behind the protective barrier of the atmosphere. The dock is flat and dark, bright white lights reflect off polished surfaces. A few of my lady's ships and another, large vessel, occupy it. Beyond the invisible seal is space. The stars are infinite, twinkling and promising life beyond the void of darkness that separates us.

We approach the vessel, a sleek black ship with an assortment of white lights. The engines turn to life and a ramp lowers from the belly to the hard cold floor of the dock. I trail my master, the chain guiding me. The ship is bigger than any other I have graced, and I fear I will get lost. But I know in my heart, it won't be a problem. There is nowhere to run in space. No escape. I will not need to know my way around. I swallow and watch my feet as we climb up the ramp. The door hisses shut behind us and they detach my helmet and gloves, taking them from me.

I don't pay attention as we navigate the narrow halls and twists and turns. I don't mind that the entourage breaks up, one by one slipping away until it is just my master and I. I am not delusional. I know my fate. I know what comes next. I am a sex slave, and now I will copulate as I have been taught to do.

But can I do it?

A door hisses open before us and I know where we are. The blue and silver decadence can only mean it is my master's personal quarters. Plush carpets. High price paintings. Tapestries depicting scenery on an ocean planet. A large bed, black sheets pulled taught, dominates the room. A massive view window, closed, takes up the right wall. An opulent powder room lies beyond a small door tucked into the corner. A desk is caddy-cornered to the bed. This ship is not meant for long journeys. This man has a much grander home waiting for us elsewhere. He only does two things in this room.

He releases my chain and detaches it as the door hisses shut behind me. I step back, hoping it will open at my presence, but I bump against cold metal. The ship vibrates under my feet as the engines turn in earnest. Varashka pulls his robes loose and drops them to the floor. Beneath he wears a spacesuit like mine, and under that his muscles are lean and taught. He faces me. His smirk irritates me, but I cannot react.

"Now, you are mine."

I inhale a shuddering breath as he unzips his suit, stopping at his navel. He approaches and loosens my hair out of the delicate bun. It cascades down my shoulders and he pushes it back. He grips me and pulls me hard against him, it is almost painful. He crushes me in his grip. Hatred, anger, penetrates the pink hue of his irises. He bends down and presses his lips with force against mine. I squeeze my eyes shut. He pushes my lips apart with his tongue. It's messy. Sloppy. He tastes like the spicy tobacco my lady uses. I tried it once. I hated it.

I whimper as he tugs me to the bed, pushing me down onto it. He crawls over me, forcing my legs apart.

"I considered taking my time with you. Drawing this out. Relishing it, but then I realized, I have all the time in the universe. I can be slow with you later."

Before I can respond, not that I will, he smothers me. The ship jolts as it takes off from the dock. I'm aware of engines rising in power and speed beneath us. Varashka's deft hands yank at the zipper of my suit. Beneath I'm bare and his hand slips to my breast. He kneads my flesh and I cannot retain a gasp. I'm scared.

He laughs against my lips and pulls away.

"Yes. That's it." He grips a fistful of my hair, pulling, yanking my head back to expose my neck to him. "I'm going to fuck you so hard," he lingers on the last two words. Drawing them out with my fear. I cannot hide it from him, and it pleases him.

The ship shudders and we bounce with the movement. It doesn't faze my master. His tongue travels around my neck. He pulls the fabric of my suit open and I blush under his scrutiny.

"Gods, you *are* perfect," he whispers. "I will treat you well."

He leans over and his long tongue glides over the soft flesh of my breasts and nipples. They rise under his attention. I whimper and dare to push against him.

"No," I find my voice. "P-please. Master."

"Hmm," he continues, his hand traveling down with the zipper past my navel.

The ship shudders again, rough. I yelp as we bounce, but this time Varashka sits up. Angry.

A moment later a chime precedes the intercom, "Sir."

"What? For fuck's sake."

"Pirates."

He growls and beats his fist into the plush mattress beside me. He rips from the bed, forgetting his half open suit, and tears from the room. The door hisses shut behind him.

I sit up, catching my breath, thankful for reprieve. I zip up my suit and tuck my legs beneath me. The ship shudders again and I lose my balance, half lying on the bed. A violent jolt and alarms sound. A robotic voice repeats a phrase over and over. It isn't in Galactic Common. I don't understand her, but the door opens of its own accord.

I wait. An eternity. Piercing gun fire echoes down the hall. The alarm continues, loud and urgent. I run to the window and search for a control panel. I find it and mash on buttons until it hisses open. Next to us is a vessel. Not as large, or sleek. It's beat up, but loaded with guns. Painted on the side, crudely, is a name in white.

"Whydah," I whisper.

The ship rocks and I lurch forward, catching myself on the window. Beams of fire blast from our ship to the other, but invisible shields block the attack. Another voice takes over the intercom, and this one I understand.

"We've been boarded. Begin measure twenty-one." My master's voice. Calm. Collected. Cold.

I run for the door as the robotic voice resumes its foreign commands. No one takes notice of me as I run through the halls. With each shudder I catch myself and keep on. I don't know where I'm going. There are no maps. No way to navigate these halls. I curse myself for not paying attention after all. How could I know? The crew are distinguishable. All in suits matching mine. Different races and species. Different builds and appearance.

I don't see pirates until I reach a cargo bay. I know this must be it. Large boxes are strapped down to walls and floors, but not all of them. Not anymore. A crew of mismatching uniforms unbuckle and roll the cargo away. A line of them watch the exits and doors, guns fired up and ready for action in their hands. Claws. Tentacles.

I lean against the doorway, watching. Waiting. The ship jolts and the crew are steady on their feet. They hardly sway as I fall. They laugh in unison, bawdy and confident, as one of their own stumbles to the metal floor. I gasp and reach out.

It's Parishioner. I eject from the doorway and wave my hands. He has difficulty getting to his feet and the pirates raise their guns at me.

"Parish!" I project over the chaos surrounding us. "Parish!"

He looks up, sweating, panting, and points to me, "That's our cargo!"

Without hesitation the pirates nod and part to let me through, training their guns on the doors again. I dash to my old man, the ship bouncing beneath my feet and even the steady have a stumble. We both fall to the floor and I crawl to him. I latch on.

"You came," I cry. "You came for me."

"Of course I did," he smiles and we get to our feet.

The ship steadies and we reach the end of the cargo bay, where bodies of my master's crew lay. I can't look at them long, not once I know they are dead. Guilt washes over me. I tell myself they must be bad. They must be. They mustn't have families at home waiting for their return.

A small transport ship lies in wait, its back door open. Other vessels are scattered close by, and beyond them is an open wall leading to space. The invisible seal keeps us alive and shields us from the hazards of the cosmos. My old man pulls me into the transport and we sit in the two seats behind the pilot. Parishioner reaches across and buckles me in before himself.

"I've got her," he says.

The pilot, hidden by the chair they occupy, reaches out a gloved hand and gives a thumb up. The door hisses shut behind us, the transport can only house three, and it hovers into the air before lurching out into space. I grow nauseas as butterflies in my stomach dance. The inertia of our flight is more prominent on a small vessel.

I grip my old man's hands. I'm so happy. I can't stop grinning at him, and him at me.

"You came," I repeat.

Tears well his blue eyes, "Of course I did."

He pats my hand and doesn't let go until we are past the shield of Whydah and slowing into her dock. It surprises me how little the ship rocks under the assault of Varashka's weaponry. The door to the transport hisses outward and Parishioner unbuckles me. I stand and wobble out onto the ramp. I drop to my knees and bend over. I'm nauseas. Thankful. I lower my forehead to the cool floor.

Behind me, Parishioner and the pilot step out.

"I wouldn't do that. Who knows the last time it was mopped."

I sit up and turn round to see Taren, our pilot. He sticks the ends of his glove between his teeth and yanks off, finger by finger. His dark gaze makes me blush, but Parishioner comes between us to help me up.

"Are you all right?" my old man asks.

I nod.

"...were we in time?"

I smile, "Yes."

"Oh, thank God." He waves his hand up, down, left, and right, like he always does. "Come on. You can stay with me."

I stop and pause, my hand in Parishioner's. I turn to the man in black.

"Thank you."

He nods, holding his gloves.

2. Samiyah

I sleep like never before.

When I wake, Parishioner snores in his chair at the desk. Our cabin is small, but there are two beds across from each other. Clothes and papers layer one, and the other is where I lay. At the opposite end of the door is the desk. On either side of the door to the hall are closets just large enough I might can stand in them, if they are empty.

I sit up. New surroundings disorient me. I forget for a moment where I am and how I got to be here. The pirate raid didn't last long after we boarded Whydah. I vaguely remember assurance that it's all under control. The raid finished before we reached our quarters and we were in hyperdrive by the time I fell asleep to Parishioner's beautiful hymns. Safe. Sound.

The butterflies in my stomach complain with hunger. I hover my hands over it and will them to quiet. I don't want to wake the old man, but I am starving. I stand and to my happy surprise the door hisses open when I step before it.

Samiyah

The hallway is empty. This ship has a different feel than the other. Not as cold and perfect. Flawed and beautiful. I brush my hand over the uneven patchwork pipes running along the corridor. It's warm. Living. Breathing. This isn't a vessel to transport, but a home.

Doors line the hallway often and I think this is where a lot of the crew lives. I pick a direction and walk with caution.

A robot, small, rolling on one wheel keeping an impossible balance as it does so, rounds the corner and stops short to avoid me. Its green eyes look into mine, mirroring my emerald with a sickly green. The gears whir beneath its metal skin.

"Can you help me?" I ask.

It nods. Robotic voice, "Yes. How may I help you sir/madam/other?"

"Can you show me food?"

Its gears whir. "Food. Yes. Follow."

It turns on the wheel beneath it and goes in the direction from which it came. I follow at a jog. It doesn't look back to make sure I am here. I can't lose it. At the end of the hall is an elevator. The door slides open after a chime and the robot pushes its way in. A group of the marauders chat, but quiet when I step inside. Their body heat radiates in the small enclosure. They are not human, so I don't know if they are male or female. Or what species. Just not like me.

The elevator stops and the robot rattles off across the grate floors. I follow without a glance back, but I can feel their eyes on me. In their various shapes, sizes, and colors. Another hallway. Another maze. This ship I may take the time to memorize, but I don't know how long we'll be here.

Another door hisses open and we step through into a large room.

"Food."

The robot turns and leaves. The chatter of the room quiets and I turn to find all eyes on me. Sitting at metal benched tables the pirates still. Forks hover mid air. Those who serve the steaming food onto trays freeze, food plopping onto the metal surface of the counter. I wring my hands and swallow. I'm accustomed to being the center of attention, but not like this. Not in the open. Not in front of so many. Not so vulnerable. I miss my lady now, more than I thought possible. Who is to keep me safe here? I shouldn't have left Parishioner in the cabin.

A woman stands. She has mammalian, human features, but similar to my master she has blue scale skin and green eyes. Her hair is striking pink and shaved at the sides into a Mohawk. Her tray is empty and as she approaches me, I feel small. She towers over me. She glances back over her shoulder to the crowd.

"Eat."

At once they get back to their meals. The chatter picks up as she puts her hand on my back and guides me to the line of food and servers.

"Here," she plucks an empty tray from the pile and hands it to me. "Put it down there. Tell them what you want."

I slide the tray along and point to what I want. The cooks, or...serving stock of this ship, say nothing as they glop my food down. It isn't fresh fruits or cut meats I'm accustomed to, but it is food and I am so hungry.

They serve the woman after me. I reach the end of the line and stand with my tray weighed down with food. The steam rises and heat wafts into my face. Despite its appearance, it smells delicious.

The woman's hand finds my back again and she guides me to a full table.

"Move," she says. The table empties. We sit alone.

She withdraws two forks from the can in the middle of the table and hands one to me.

I nod, "Thank you. For your kindness."

She eyes me and starts eating, shoveling food into her mouth as quickly as she can.

I eat with the slow, thoughtful manners I was taught. She finishes long before I do, but waits. With patience she picks at her teeth with her fork and keeps others from prying.

I set down my utensil, my food half eaten. I rest my hands in my lap.

"May I ask your name?" I ask.

She rolls her eyes, "Setsui."

I open my mouth, but she raises her hand.

"I know. Samiyah."

"Oh." I look around, catching stares.

"I don't think there's a soul on board who doesn't know of you. They're just pleasantly surprised to find the rumors are true."

"I see," I sigh.

"You're used to this."

"Yes," I shrink in my seat. "But under different circumstances."

She cracks a smile, "Don't worry. No one on board will mess with you. They may stare a bit, but no one will touch you."

I offer a smile. This makes me feel better.

"Captain don't tolerate that type on board. And if he finds them, it ain't pretty. He gets creative."

I swallow and look down at the worn clean surface of the metal table.

"I don't envy you. Bet you don't hear that much," she stacks our trays.

"Actually, I do."

She raises her black brows and leans back, "Well, are you done?"

I nod.

"Good. I think captain wants to see you before the old man wakes up."

I've never been to the bridge of a ship before now. The door opens up into a wide room with dozens of control panels lighting up the dim space. Half of them have operators, while the others seem to be in a state of suspense.

The view window expands across the entire width of the bridge. Before it I catch a familiar silhouette. Setsui leads me to him and, unsure of how to greet him, I bow to Taren. Beyond the viewing window lies a planet below our orbit. Blue oceans surround green and lush land mass. I approach the window and place my hands against it, willing to touch the swirling water and leaves below.

"Like home planet," I whisper.

Taren is beside me, his close presence sends a shiver down my spine as always.

"Yes. Have you ever been?" he asks.

I shake my head.

"We need to discuss something."

I swallow and tear my gaze from the scenery below.

His black eyes search mine.

"Would you like to go down there?" he asks.

I nod, "Very much so."

"Good. I need you to—"

"Sir."

Taren turns to his crewmember. Red and black fur covers a humanoid of short stature from head to toe.

"We have an incoming message from general Varashka."

My heart leaps into my throat and I tense. Taren glances sideways at me and nods to his man.

"Go ahead."

A small portion of the viewing window disappears beneath a small black square. An image of my master's face overlays until it appears three dimensional.

He snarls, "Give. Her. Back."

I wait for Taren's response, but he only crosses his arms.

The screen goes black, disappears, and the viewing window is back to normal. I open my mouth, to say something, anything, but find no words.

"That was the message?" he asks.

The red man nods, "Yep. That's it."

A message. How foolish of me. In deep space a response can take several hours.

"Funny," Taren continues, "No mention of the hundreds of thousands of speks worth of cargo we took."

He turns to me, "How much did he pay for you?"

"Six million," I answer, looking down.

He nods. "Impressive. You don't seem proud."

"Would you be?"

"I suppose not." He waves his hand over the viewing window, "This is our destination. Blufiga

Five. I need Sylvester, or Parishioner as you like to call him, to do something for me here."

Taren places his arm around my shoulder. His touch is warm. Inviting. I withhold my gasp.

"We made a deal. A bargain. I picked you up, now he has to do what I want. And what do I want?"

"No touching," I remind him with a whisper.

"Right," he drops his arm. "Apologies. And what I want is for him to translate something for me. No technology works there. It's a dead zone. I can't take a picture. It's too big and...weird for me to copy it to paper myself. He just needs to be there, but now he's reluctant. See, I got you for him. Risked Varashka's wrath. Lady Cademe's, so to speak, and now he wants to back out. He's afraid for you, and your safety. And really, it's not a terribly dangerous place. It's not so bad. I just need you to tell him how much you want to go there."

I can only focus on one thing, from the message, "He's a general?"

"Not really. It's just a name he's acquired. He's...hmm. How to put it?"

"A mercenary," Setsui pipes in behind us.

I forgot she is here.

"He's built himself a bit of an empire. Very capable. I'm sure he's dangerous, but not really my concern. Or yours. I've had worse mad at me than him. I'm sure he'll get over you."

I smile, but I'm not sure of this.

"Can you do this for me? Can you convince Sylvester to take you down there? He doesn't want to leave you here alone, but he doesn't want you going down. I think it best if we just, all go together."

I ponder. "And you want me to go so that I'm a hostage? So that you can use me to get your way if he's reluctant?"

Taren clicks his tongue and cocks his brow, "I'm impressed you can form complicated sentences. I wont lie, I wondered."

He's changing the subject, and I know I'm right.

"What will happen if I do not convince him?"

The pirate captain sighs and steps before me, caging me between his arms against the viewing screen. I lean back against the cool, hard surface.

"Well, nothing bad will happen to *you*. You're too valuable."

My breath quickens. "But you will hurt him? My Parishioner?"

"Will I?" he shrugs.

I think of how I want to do this as I follow Setsui down the maze of halls. We stop in front of a door. Parishioner's I assume. I have an idea and thank her. I step through and Parishioner naps in his chair, but the snoring has ceased. I sigh and sit on the empty bed.

"Parish?" I whisper.

He smacks his lips. His glasses hang loose in his hand.

I stand and lean over him, shaking his shoulder.

His eyes flutter open and he puts on his glasses. He looks up at me.

"Oh, oh yes. How are you?"

I smile, "Fine. You?"

"Oh good. Good." He sighs and swivels in the chair, his back to me.

I must begin. Taren insists Parishioner doesn't know of our conversation. The way my old man is, I think it wise. I know he would be angry and refuse to do anything. I worry for myself, of course, but also him. I think I preferred it when I knew he was safe and sound. I thought they were friends, but maybe a pirate can never really have them. Either way, it's too late now.

"Parish?" I ask.

"Hmm? Yes?" He stands and stretches, sits back down.

"I'm…scared."

He swivels to me with knit brows, "Why my dear?"

"I don't know these…pirates. And I wonder if we are safe from my master."

Parishioner waves his finger at me, "You don't have a master anymore. Never again."

"But…" I pause, opening my hands to him. "Are we safe?"

"Yes. Oh yes. We are in very capable hands."

I nod and smile, empty. "Good. Although," I'm awful for manipulating him like this, "It means we must stay where we are. Stay with your friend, right?"

Parishioner sighs and takes off his glasses, wiping them with his shirt.

"Yes. I'm afraid so. But only for a time."

"Is my…is Varashka looking for me? I think he is."

Parishioner nods, "I'm afraid that must be true too."

I smile, "But we are safe here. Together."

"Yes," he mirrors me. "We are. Now I must…go talk to Taren. I'll be back shortly. Don't you worry about a thing and I'll bring you some supper."

Samiyah

I wait with an upset stomach. I discover one of the closet doors leads to a powder room and I sit next to it, holding my mid section, anticipating sickness. I don't experience it often. My lady was sure that any who visited me were in peak physical health. Only when another stock was sick did I catch anything.

Sweat beads my forehead. It isn't only sickness. I'm nervous. I think back to the bridge, when Taren leaned in so close. I could feel the heat of his breath. I wonder if I have exchanged one prison for another. How long will we have to do as he says?

The door hisses open and Parishioner huffs past me. He's upset. He sits down on the bed covered in his things and some of them slide off onto the floor around him.

"I don't want to go to that bloody planet."

I wipe my forehead, "What is it?"

"He wants me to go down there and I don't want to."

"Who?" I know. Liar.

"Taren."

I notice he forgets my supper. Not that I want any food. The thought raises nausea up my throat and I cover my mouth.

"Shouldn't we do as he asks?" I swallow bile.

Parishioner sighs, "*We* aren't doing anything. You're staying here."

I shake my head. I don't have to be convincing now. This is real.

"No, please. Don't leave me again." I stand, "What if he finds me? What if he attacks while you are gone? I'm not safe without you."

My old man's face softens. There is no need to explain who "he" is.

"That planet is dangerous."

"But if Taren is so strong, as you say, then it shouldn't matter. If he can protect us from Varashka, why can't he protect us from the planet?"

Parishioner's brows furrow. "Yes. I suppose you're right. It may be better if you come with us. I trust Taren, but—"

And I think you shouldn't, Parishioner.

"I don't know his crew very well."

He turns to the papers on the bed and sifts through them. "I need to gather my things and we'll go."

I braid my hair back as he gathers parchments and books. I recognize the writing on papers he stuffs into a leather pack.

"Fjordooli?" I ask.

"Ah, yes," he smiles. "Do you remember everything I taught you on it?"

I nod, "Of course. I remember everything you've told me."

He glances down at his papers, then back to me. "Everything?"

"Yes."

"Then we won't need all this." He pulls papers out of his bag and selects a handful. He rolls them and slides them back in. Then adds a small book.

I bend down and pick up the mess that slid from the bed. I know the writings. I can read and recall their meanings. Yes. I remember it all. In my spare time, what else could I do? Singing and dancing were like second nature to me. I needed something else to occupy my mind. But no one ever thinks of my mind. No one except Parishioner.

Samiyah

I stare out the viewing window on the bridge. Taren and Parishioner talk in whispers behind me. A chime rings in and a button on the panel below the viewing window blinks.

Taren steps forward and leans over to push it.

The black screen appears and my master takes up the space. His hair is unkempt. His pink eyes evolve to crimson. Blood covers his suit and hands.

"I'm warning you," he sneers. "Give her back to me. You've no idea what I've done to get her. What I will do to get her back. I will find you. Hunt you. I can. And I will."

He fists his hands, driving long nails into his own palms. I wince, knowing those nails may penetrate my own skin someday.

Taren watches my reaction and turns back to the screen.

"She, is mine," Varashka repeats in a growl.

The screen goes black and disappears. I stare where it was, not seeing the blue swirling ocean beneath.

The man in black places his hand on my shoulder. I want to shy away, but I enjoy his warmth too much. I tear my eyes away from the ocean to look into his.

"He can't, Samiyah." This is only the second time he says my name. It's different than the first. There's a feeling to it. As though he realizes it is the name of a person, and not a thing.

I nod, but I am not sure. Behind us Parishioner huffs, shifting his bag to the other shoulder.

"We better get a move on. The sooner we leave, the sooner we can get back and get out of here. We're sitting ducks."

Taren keeps his black eyes on me. His warm hand slides from my shoulder.

"Do you want to have a go at him?" he asks.

My dark brows furrow, "What?"

"Do you want to have some fun?"

Parishioner steps forward, "I'm not sure that's wise."

Taren flicks his hand to silence him.

"Relax old man."

I ponder, chewing on my inner cheek. I want to please Taren. Our fate rests in his hands.

"All right," I say.

Parishioner sighs.

Taren smiles, "That a girl. C'mon." He turns and we stumble after him.

My old man labors. Breathing heavy. Sweat rolls down his face.

I slow to accommodate his speed, and in turn Taren looks over his shoulder and does the same. I don't know this part of the ship and we step through a door. The room is bigger than ours by spades. To the right of the door is an unmade double bed with a desk at the foot. A screen lights up the surface. Above the bed is an open viewing window. Instead of the planet it's the dark twinkling of space. To the left of the door is a large screen taking up the wall. A map of our surroundings. The local solar system. Beacons, small, with lettering, move across it. Other ships. Stations. A radar such as this is illegal, but its presence doesn't surprise me. A dresser is tucked into the corner, drawers half open with black clothes spilling out.

"This is your room," I say.

Taren nods. Parishioner leans against the door frame. His complexion pales and I fear he'll be sick. Taren points to an open door next to the dresser. A powder room.

Samiyah

"Thank you. Just some space sickness," my old man nods and sets down his bag, excusing himself. The door hisses shut behind him and I am alone with the man in black.

Taren walks over to the desk and with a touch of his finger the screen rises to face the bed. He gestures to the rumpled sheets.

"I'll need to touch you," he whispers.

The thought excites me. Butterflies dance in my stomach.

"But not much?" I ask.

He smiles, "Only as much as you want me to. You can tell me to stop at any time."

I nod, "What do you want me to do?"

He reaches down to the hem of his black tunic, pulling it over his head. His muscles flex with the movement and I resist the urge to smooth my hands over dips and grooves of his chest and stomach. I swallow as he keeps his eyes on mine, fighting the instinct to study his body as so many have mine.

He sits on the bed, facing the screen, and I realize it has a camera. It mirrors his image on its hard surface. I watch him on the screen, waving me over.

"Sit here", he crosses his legs and pats the space before them.

My heart leaps into my throat. This is different from my master. My body is warm. I obey, crawling onto the bed, and I sit in front of him, my back to his chest.

"We're not going to say anything," Taren instructs, pulling my hair loose from the braid.

His hands trail slow through my hair, warm against my scalp. So intimate. Soft. I wonder if this is how he would undress me. Slow. With purpose.

I let out a held breath and nod.

"Tell me to stop, when you want me to," he whispers in my ear.

I close my eyes. I don't want him to.

"Record," he says.

The screen chimes and a red light blinks in the bottom corner.

I watch our reflection. His hands splay over my stomach, pulling me back into his lap. His bulge is warm against my backside. As his deft fingers slide the zipper of my suit down to my navel, it hardens. My eyes hood in the screen. I like this. I lean my head back against his shoulder as his hand dips beneath my suit, his thumb brushing along the underside of my breast. His breath hitches, his bulge straining against the leather of his pants. He likes it as much as I.

His lips ghost along my jaw and ear. Shivers coat my skin. I turn to face him. Our lips brush, then meet. He's soft. Gentle. A stark contrast to Varashka. Taren's arms tighten around me. I forget the screen. My master. Even Parishioner. Everything. There is only his kiss, his breath, his warm hands.

"What in God's name are you two doing?" Parishioner stands in the open doorway, leaning against it.

We startle and my skin cools without Taren's touch. He zips up my suit without a word and slides from behind me. He pulls on his shirt.

"End recording. Edit out last five seconds," the computer chimes and the blinking light stops. "Send message to Caligula."

I catch my breath, sitting up straight, watching Parishioner approach the man in black.

"I said don't touch her," he pokes the younger man in the chest.

Taren smiles. It's easy, light.

Samiyah

"I asked permission. It's a gag. For our dear old friend, Varashka."

Parishioner shifts his stare to me, "He had your permission?"

Under his gaze shame washes over me in a blush. Heat covers my cheeks.

I nod, "Yes."

"All right," he says, but I don't think it is.

The transport shuttle lands rough in a clearing. It's bigger, and a crew of ten fits. Parishioner and myself take up two of those slots. The other eight are well prepared. Guns. Both electric and manual. Knives. Machetes. A pocket size weapon that makes you shake. My lady used it on me once. And once was enough. She always used it on the stock who misbehaved. She called it her shocker, but the pirates call it a Taser.

Setsui comes with us. This makes me happy. I do like her, even if she doesn't like me. I think she might though. She shows me kindness when she doesn't have to.

When the door to the shuttle whirs open, steam dampens my braided hair and exposed skin. The spacesuit protects the rest of me from such heat. I wave my hand in front of my face, but excitement drives me out of the shuttle first. Taren snatches my hand and jerks me behind him. He points his finger down, stern.

"Stay behind me. You don't go first," he says.

Embarrassing. I nod, "I'm sorry."

"Don't be sorry," he sighs. "It's for safety. You don't know what's out here." He points to the thicket beyond.

The thicket. I forget him, my old man, everything, when I step out onto the plush carpet of forest floor after him. I squat down and push my hands against the spongy surface. My fingers curl into the moss and vines. So green. So soft. The crew finishes their preparations and close the door to the transport.

Parishioner straps his bag to his shoulders, resting it against his back. I walk with him, in the middle of the group, and take his sweaty hand.

"Are you all right?" I ask him, as he asks me so many times in my life.

"Oh," he's out of breath already, "I'm fine dear. I'm just an old man who's out of shape." He pats my hand in his, "Nothing to worry about."

I nod with a smile and study our surroundings. A thick canopy of trees shade us from the hot sun. Birds tweet, mammals whoop in the distance. Flowers bloom high above from trunks covered in moss and in little bundles at their base. The leaves we crush beneath our feet are moist and silent.

"Is this like home planet?" I ask.

Parishioner smiles, "Yes. Parts of it."

My old man draws me close, his breath huffing.

"Samiyah," he begins.

I nod, listening.

"I don't want you to get too close to Taren. He can be..." he swallows. Takes a breath, "He can be smooth with the ladies. I don't think he will treat you right. Treasure you for who you really are. He can be false."

Shame heats my face. I know he thinks of the kiss. It was real for me. I liked it. I want more of it, but I lie to him and myself.

"Do not worry. It was really for the joke. I think it will be funny."

A whir of powering down grabs my attention. Electric guns around us go black and silent. Dead.

Taren sighs, "And here we are. Switch to manual."

His followers do as they're told, tucking their useless weaponry back into their belts before withdrawing ancient guns. Ones that use bullets. We leave one crewmember behind for messages from Whydah, and trudge forward through the curtain of thicket following Taren and his machete.

I see nothing beyond the brush. Parishioner gasps beside me, squeezing my hand. He leans on me, using myself to keep him upright.

"We need to stop," I say. "My Parishioner needs rest."

We don't, however. Taren glances back over his shoulder, sweating and panting himself, "Nearly there."

He doesn't lie, in minutes we break through the thicket he chops at tirelessly. We come out into a clearing and before us is a high cliff face. At the bottom of it, a sealed doorway looms. An open gap in the canopy above creates a tunnel of light, shining a beam down on the ancient stone. I can read the writing swirling from the inside outward. Parishioner stops and drops to his knees. I squat beside him as he shoos me away.

"I'm fine," he can barely breathe. "Go have a look."

I stay, but he pushes me forward.

"Go on now."

I approach the stone. A whisper breathes outward from it in a cool breeze. Loose wisps of hair tickle my face. Taren places his hand on the rock.

"Feel it?" he asks.

I nod and raise my hand to trace the symbols of Fjordooli. Taren watches my hand.

"Hmm," I stop at an unfamiliar combination of marks. I figure it out in context.

Taren cocks his brow, "Can you read that?"

I nod.

"Captain!" the alien crewmember we left behind crashes from the thicket. "Varashka's in hyperspace. Thirty minutes out from Whydah."

"Fuck," Taren whispers. He turns to Parishioner, "You need to move it old man."

I worry, laying my hand on my chest. My master is angry. Our joke infuriates him. I will suffer. We all will.

"Sylvester?" Taren calls.

I turn to find Parishioner collapsing, still, lifeless on the forest floor.

I dive to him, shake him.

"Parish?" I cry. "Parishioner?" Tears blur my vision. "I told you he needed rest," my voice rises with panic. "Rest."

Taren snaps his fingers and Setsui kneels beside me. She checks his mouth, his wrists.

"I have a pulse. Weak. Without a reader, I don't know what's going on." She pulls a small, dead, square from her pocket. She shakes it.

The man in black takes hold of my wrist and drags me to the stone.

"You said you can read it," he pants. Sweat rolls down his face and neck. "Read it for me."

I glance back over my shoulder to my old man. Setsui leans over him, her ear to his mouth.

"The faster you read it, the faster we leave," Taren coaxes. He pulls out a pad of paper and pencil. Archaic, but effective. "Write it down."

I take them and look up to the words. In my panic they blur.

"Hurry," a crewmember whines.

The others put together a gurney for my old man as I translate. I write down the jumble of words, my hands shake. Taren watches me, glancing upward to the break in canopy that allows the sunlight to shine down over the doorway.

"This isn't a doorway," I whisper. "This is no door." I finish and return the pad of paper.

"Didn't think so," he tucks it into the satchel hanging off of his shoulder to his hip.

We flee. Setsui and three others carry my Parishioner, and I run beside them. Beneath my suit, sweat coats my skin. It rolls down my back, beneath the hair of my scalp, and the slightest breeze cools it. The guns whir to life from the bags and belts of the crew when we leave the dead zone. We follow the rough cut path Taren formed on our journey and soon reach the shuttle. We clamor in, my old man lying strapped to the gurney on the floor. Setsui leans over him, her small device attaches to his cheek.

"Heart failure," she looks up at Taren as he straps into the pilot's chair, retrieving a first aid case.

"Buckle," and everyone does as he says, including me.

They hook straps down against the floor over my old man and when we launch out of orbit he is immobile. Tears stream my cheeks. I bite my manicured nails. He told me some cycles ago this can happen. But I am not ready.

3. Samiyah

He dies, in my arms, in the infirmary. The room is cold. White and sterile. He can't die here. He should die on home planet. I inhale a shuddering breath and hold him to me.

"Please," I whisper. "Please don't leave me alone." I fist his hair and squeeze him against me. "Please."

I know I am not pretty as I cry. My face is red, swollen with grief, twisting. I want to be angry with Taren, but he did not make my old man die. His heart did. It gave up. Perhaps it is better his last sight was of green and blue like home planet.

The pirate leans against the doorway, his face expressionless. Somber. He rubs it several times. Setsui sits beside me. Her frown quivers. Her eyes glassy.

Shame constricts my chest. I think he dies disappointed in me.

I sniff and lay him down on the hard metal table. I brush grey hair from his wrinkled face. His smile will never comfort me again. His gentle touch. His incessant, wonderful questions after my wellbeing.

Samiyah

I lay over him, resting my face in my hands over his chest. I have never lost like this. Never.

I grip his hand, still warm, but cooling. His life leaves his body. I hope his soul returns to home planet, where he was happiest.

Setsui excuses herself, leaving me with Taren standing next to me.

"Can we," I hiccup, "Take him to home planet?"

The man in black sighs. "Home planet is no more Samiyah. Earth was destroyed years ago."

"No, please." I shake my head, "This can't be true."

"It is."

I wail. Where will my old man go? Taren pulls me away. I reach for my Parishioner, and find the youthful warmth of the pirate instead. He grips me. Holds me to him. He shudders in silent tears. We cry together, dropping to our knees.

"I'm sorry," he whispers into my hair. "I'm sorry."

I press my face against his chest, curling up in his embrace. He rocks me until I can cry no more.

I wake beneath soft sheets. Cotton. Worn. Grey.

I blink, finding myself in Taren's room. In his bed. He sits at the desk at the foot of the bed, cross-legged.

Out of habit I sit up, searching for my Parishioner. My face twists into a dry cry when I realize he is gone. Forever. My old man is no more. I hug the plush pillow and sit up.

Taren spares a glance over his shoulder. Past him I read my own handwriting on the screen. He took a picture of the paper pad.

I curl my legs beneath me, shielding myself from Taren with the pillow as he turns round to face me, leaning back against the desk.

He studies me, quiet.

"What," my throat is dry. I force the words, "What are you going to do with me?"

Taren cocks his head to the side, "Nothing."

"You're not going to sell me?" I ask.

He shakes his head, "I made a promise. I intend to keep it." He lowers his gaze, whispering, "Especially now."

I know I should find relief, but none comes. My stomach knots.

His lips tighten, and relax.

"What?" he asks.

I hide half of my face behind the pillow, squeezing it. I am a woman, but I feel like a child. In his hands. Helpless.

"You said you would hurt him."

He scoffs and looks down at his bare feet, a paper white contrast to his black clothes, shaking his head.

"I lied. I would never hurt him. I used you to get him to do what I wanted." He glances up, "I'm sorry."

"Used me." Parishioners warning words, some of his last, haunt me. "He said you will. You are smooth and false. You see me not as you should."

"I see you as valuable," he admits. "But not for the reason you think."

He leans forward and I shy away from his touch, leaning back against the wall. He crawls, sitting next to me. The warmth of his thigh touches mine.

"You can read Fjordooli. That is worth far more to me than beauty."

This doesn't comfort. I watch him, waiting.

"I know how you feel," he says. "I always wonder if people want me for me. Or for who I am. And I know you don't know who I am. If you did I think..." He takes a deep breath. "You would be more afraid than you are now. But it doesn't matter, I am who I am."

"Why?" I whisper. "Should I be afraid of you?"

"No," he shakes his head. "No. Something I do know, is he loved you like his own child. His own daughter. And I will honor his memory, forever. I would dishonor us both beyond redemption if I lead you to harm."

"So you will keep me safe from—" My breathe catches. I scramble over his lap to look out the window. The planet is nowhere. The stars are lines as we travel through hyperspace.

"We're safe," he rests his hand on the back of my calf. "While you were seeing to Parishioner, we left. Varashka is far behind us."

I sit back, his hand slides from my calf. I look down to my wringing hands.

"You risk your crew for this. For me."

Taren gauges his words and presses a loose wisp of hair behind my ear.

"Not really. We know what we're doing. We all do. And I asked them. Put it to a vote. I do nothing like this without their blessing. Sylvester was worth it. Now you are."

"And you will use me," I say.

"Yes," he drops his hand. "As you will use me."

Words catch in my throat. He is right. I use him for protection. Food. Shelter. This is mutual, as Parishioner would say. Oh Parishioner.

I can't breathe again. His loss leaves me empty. Hollow.

"You don't understand," my mouth is wet. My head pulses in pain from tears that can't come. "He is all I have. You have your crew. I have no one."

Taren sighs and takes my hands in his. I let him, my chest shuddering in sobs. I watch his pale hands encase mine, our skins a contrast of color.

"You have me," he says.

I don't know where we are going. And I don't care. Taren wants me to read for him again, and I will. I have no choice. I have nowhere else to be. To go. Nothing else to do. And he's right. He is all I have. I leave the safety of his room only to visit my Parishioner. He is frozen, still, in a cryogenic chamber. Taren says he has special plans for him. He thinks I'll like it.

Taren touches me little. Only my shoulder or hands. Sometimes, in the night, when I watch the stars in the window and he sleeps on a pallet by the bed, I want to roll over and stroke his face. His hair. He may be false, but I cannot help myself. I have seen many false aliens and people in my life, and none are as skillful as he. None can convince me as he has. I wonder, when alone, if he came to me before at the ranch and asked me to run away with him, would I have said yes? Would I have risked my lady's wrath to be with him?

I think so.

I remember the ranch. The sun and breeze. I haven't felt a wind in many cycles. Not since the stone that breathed out to us. Not since Parishioner's death.

Samiyah

I pile Parishioner's things around me on the bed.
Through the view window a space station thrives.
Alive. Ships fly in and out. A blinking rainbow of
lights comes and goes in waves around its spheres
and passages. We docked two cycles ago. The pirates
resupply. Have their fun, but I stay here. It is quiet on
the ship without them. I organize and read through
Parishioner's belongings. Many are Fjordooli. Things
I already know. Some are the holy book he loved so
much and interpretations with notes. Some are
letters from the past. I don't read those. They are not
my business. Instead I file them away in a box Taren
gave me. He says to hold onto them. There is no rush.

Taren is on the station. Has been since our
docking, but I do not worry. Setsui promised me she
would keep an eye on him when they left. I think she
is my friend. I like her. She will keep him safe.

The screen of the desk rises up from the flat
surface. This usually happens when a message for
Taren comes in from the bridge.

Before I can speak, his third mate, Donnen, a
small man with a big heart covered in red and black
fur, "Samiyah."

It is the first time he speaks my name. I listen.

"A message has come for you from Varashka."

My breath catches and I crumple the paper of
Parishioner's writings in my hand.

"It's addressed to you, not the captain."

Donnen looks around in the dim bridge.

"Do you want to see it? Or should we wait?"

I swallow and shake my head, "We don't know
when he'll return. Show me."

I do not need Taren to hold my hand with every
message.

Donnen nods and licks his hairy lips.

"I have to warn you it's…graphic."

"Show me."

He doesn't have to do as I say. I am no one on this ship, but he does as I ask.

On the small screen of Taren's desk, in this intimate setting, Varashka's face appears. I feel vulnerable.

My master is in his chambers. The place where I was. He sits on the bed he forced me onto. I can only think of what he imagines to do with me there. His hair is combed back from his blue angular face. His spacesuit is pressed and laundered. He looks fresh. The pink returns to his eyes.

But kneeling in front of him is a crying crewmember. In Varashka's calm demeanor, this man's melts. He cries out in a language I don't understand.

"Samiyah," my master commands my attention. Though he cannot see me. Though he does not know I watch.

"Come back to me, my love." He smooths down the messy hair of the mostly human in front of him. "Come back to me."

I tremble when he grips the man's hair, as he did mine, and exposes his neck. Varashka slips a knife from his belt.

"This man," he runs the blunt of the blade along his captive's jaw, "is the one who was supposed to watch you. He was ordered to stay by our door. Keep you safe. I can only imagine the terrors you face in that hellhole. With that…pirate. I can only hope your purity is intact when I get you back."

The blade turns and slices across the tender flesh of the man's neck.

I gasp and drop the paper, covering my mouth with my hands. I don't understand. Why does he feel this way? Tears drop from my eyes. I do not know. How can I live with knowing a man dies because of me? I should have stayed. Maybe if I stayed he would be alive. My Parishioner might be too.

Red blood spills down the victim's neck and Varashka dips his blue fingers into it. They glisten as he lifts them to his elongated tongue. He opens his mouth to speak again, but the door hisses open and Taren dives to the bed, shutting off the screen.

"Dammit, Dennon," he mutters. He punches buttons and the red third mate answers.

"Don't give her any more messages!" the captain's voice rises.

The screen lowers flat on the desk.

Taren pants. He turns to me. I know I must be pale. Shaking. Scared.

"I think you should give me to him. He will hunt me forever."

He shakes his head and takes hold of my upper arms, "No. No."

I insist.

"Listen to me," he smooths my hair down and away from my face. "Space is vast."

I shake my head, "I don't want to run forever. I don't want to put you through this forever."

"I can kill him," he offers. His eyes brighten. He is serious.

"No," I shake my head again.

"What do you want?" he whispers.

I think. What *do* I want? Two things, but I can only say one aloud.

"To be free."

But we both know, he cannot let me go.

We leave the space station. Its bright lights disappear in an instant as we move through hyperspace. Every time I close my eyes a vision of blood gushing down a man's throat haunts me. I can't sleep. In the darkness of the room Taren slumbers on his palette. Guilt makes the butterflies in my stomach dance. My problems trouble him. I know it. He tries to keep it from me. He tosses and turns in his sleep. Like I do so many times, and I know how inappropriate it is, I roll onto my side and watch him.

He sleeps in his clothes. For my comfort. He kicks the sheets and blankets off. His mouth is open and breath heaves in and out of him in a rhythmic song of whisper.

I sit up in bed and close the viewing window, blocking out the racing stripes of stars we pass by. The room is dark but for the glowing lights of panels on the window and desk, by the doors. I hug my knees.

We're heading to our next destination. Another place I must read Fjordooli. Taren says it is dangerous. Far more than the planet like home planet. Or Earth, as he called it. Is it really Earth? My parents told me of home planet when I was young, and Parishioner, but none of them use this name. Maybe because everyone knows of Earth and her destruction. Even I. I suppose it is easier to pretend that our home planet is out there somewhere. Waiting for our return.

I rest my head on my arms.

Taren stirs and though I can't see him well, I feel his movement. He sits up and stumbles to the powder room. The fluorescent light above the sink flickers on at a dim setting, spilling into the room, and he splashes his face with water. I watch as he leans on the sink, washing his face and drinking from the tap. He turns and sees me.

"Did I wake you?" when groggy his voice is deep and scratchy.

"No," I shake my head. "I can't sleep."

He hesitates and runs his hand through his dark, thick hair.

"Did I snore?"

I can't help a smile, "No."

He yawns and the light goes out as he stumbles back to the bed, but instead of lying on his palette, he sits on the edge of the mattress close to me.

"Nervous?" he asks.

His proximity in the dark is what flutters my butterflies. I fumble for the button to the viewing window and it slides open. He blinks against the star stripes, but focuses back on me. His black eyes are haunting in this near darkness.

I cock my head to the side, "Can you see in the dark?"

"Almost. I need some light, but yes. I have the ability to see well in the dark."

His gaze drops down and climbs up to my eyes, "I can see you perfectly."

I blush. I want to touch him. Want his lips on my skin, his hands on my hips. I swallow, remembering my Parishioner's warning. He is false. He does not treasure me as he should. I do not want to disappoint my old man's soul as I did his mind in life.

"Goodnight," I slip down into the sheets.

Taren slides down from the bed and arranges his palette.

I lie awake all night.

Three cycles pass and we are in orbit over a white planet. We watch it from the bridge as the crew readies our gear. I place my fingers on the cold glass. Beneath swirls torrents of snow and wind. Ice and rolling seas lay below, cracking and shifting the crust of glaciers.

Taren takes a deep breath and exhales, "This will be like the last. Our technology will die. The stone is beneath the waves. Not far, but far enough. We'll have to use old methods."

Setsui crosses her arms next to me, "The diving bell? Are we really using that?"

"We can use our suits if you prefer to take the risk beneath an ocean."

She shakes her head.

We dress into wetsuits. I pull mine on with Setsui's assistance. Having enough help getting dressed in the past, it does not bother me to be naked in front of another. But with Taren, I don't know. I don't want him to see. Not until I'm ready.

Skin tight material, a Gnolian invention I think, covers me head to toe. It allows my fingers and toes their natural dexterity while moving through frigid water. I twirl my hair up into a net and pin it to my scalp before pulling the hood of my suit on. We all look silly and share a small laugh as we load into our shuttle. This one is larger than the last and we have to take a moment to attach the large metal bell in the cargo bay before we descend down to the planet. The crew is bigger too, I'm not sure how many, but at least three times more than the twin of home planet. We break the atmosphere and high winds whip us around. I curl my legs inward and grip my belt. Everyone else talks with excitement. The thing we seek draws near, and I don't bother to ask what it is.

Some great treasure I have no use for. I do as I'm told to survive another day off the ranch. Another day without Parishioner.

We land on solid rock after setting the bell down on ice and wailing wind whips around our shuttle, but it only vibrates. There is no threat of being blown away. If there is, I suppose we won't leave it. We all put on our helmets and check the seals. Setsui helps me with mine. The air isn't hospitable either. The door hisses open and lowers down to a ramp. Waves of methane rise into the cabin. The white snow blinds us. Taren unbuckles himself and pushes me down as I stand.

"No," he yells over the wind through the helmet's comm. "We need to set up. Switch out the methane for oxygen in the bell. Attach it to pulleys. Stay in here until I get you."

I nod and sit back down. The rest of the crew files out carrying equipment. The eternal blizzard of this planet blows and howls beyond the shelter of the shuttle. I sit for longer than I expect, but Taren's silhouette appears in the doorway, waving me forward. I follow him out. He takes hold of my hand, the wind pushes against me. I have trouble walking and he anchors me.

We leave solid ground and step on thick ice. In places it breaks by the waves of the ocean beneath, but on stable pieces we have our equipment. A large circular hole is cut into the sheet of ice and I watch as crewmembers hook grapples onto the edge before attaching themselves and dropping down, disappearing into the water. We approach one and I seize up. Taren turns to me.

"Hold onto me," he reaches between us and attaches our suits with a strap hooked onto our belts as we face each other.

My body molds against his as he fumbles with the other strap attached to the grappling hook behind my back. His arms are on either side of me, holding onto the strap as he backs up to the edge of the ice. I panic and wrap my arms around him, squeezing. We drop down into the dark water and I pant. The glass of my helmet fogs.

"Samiyah," Taren's voice is soft in the quiet beneath the waves. "Look at me."

I swallow and meet his eyes past the condensation. My breathing evens out. I think only of him looking at me. The fog clears with my head and now, the darkness is beautiful with our suits lighting up like stars in the night sky. Beneath the waves is quiet and calm. The guiding lights of our rope swim by as we lower. Below illumination outlines the circular base of the bell.

The headlamps of other crewmembers waiting for us, floating next to the bell, light our way. Taren tightens his grip on the rope and we bounce to a gentle stop. Setsui's helmet lights up her face as she comes from the darkness and detaches me from Taren. Without his grip I panic and kick my limbs. Setsui's hand finds mind and she clutches me.

"I got ya," she says with a smile.

We swim down and up into the bell. We break water and she guides me to a seat welded onto the side. Taren follows, and now it's only the three of us. The crew doesn't join us.

Taren checks a pouch attached to his thigh, unzipping it, ensuring the flares are accounted for. He seals it back up and gives a thumbs up to Setsui. My hand lingers to my own pouch. A special underwater pencil and paper pad snuggle up to my flares.

I take deep breaths. I know what I must do. We went over it a dozen times, but nothing prepares me for the panic rising with my heartbeat. The bell jolts and my head swims as we lower towards the floor of the ocean. We are close to the coast, and we don't go too far, but as Taren said it will be far enough. As predicted, our helmets and lights lining the inside of the bell die. We are cast into darkness.

A flare sparks to life beside me in Taren's hand. He holds it between his knees as he removes his helmet. He hangs the helmet on a freshly welded hook above him before reaching over to take mine. Setsui pulls off hers. It is now I notice the metal helmets with small panes of circular glass and hoses trailing out from the back strapped down to the seat.

The flare dies and we sit in darkness again. I count to eight, breathing in and out as Taren tells me to do. Our air is limited. I must not consume more than I have to.

Taren's hand finds mine and he holds it.

"Relax. We'll be in and out," his voice echoes in the bell.

I sidle close to him on the seat. The bell stops with a shudder, hitting the floor of the ocean.

Taren lights up a second flare, red light casting dancing shadows on the walls of the bell. Setsui takes it from him as the bell lifts up the height of a man from the ocean floor and stops again. We bob a moment. Setsui now lights up a second flare and Taren unstraps the metal helmet next to him. Setsui holds the flare between her sharp teeth as she unties a coiled rope attached to the bell. She slides into the water, keeping her head above the surface, and attaches it to my belt. She then unfurls another rope and attaches it to Taren as he wrestles the metal helmet free. He ticks his head towards the water and I slide down next to Setsui. Even with the protection of my Gnolian suit, splashes of water freeze like ice bullets on my cheeks. I shiver at the thought of such a deadly force kept at bay by a thin sheet of fabric encasing me.

Taren lowers the metal helmet onto my shoulders, fastening it. Setsui checks the hose seals attached to my helmet as I sink beneath its weight. I lower into the darkness, breathing the air of the bell through the hose attached to my helmet. Beyond the light glow of the lit flare coming from the bell above is perpetual darkness. The sand beneath is gray and soft. My feet sink down into it and it covers the top of my toes.

The man in black drops down next to me, his own helmet attached, with a javelin in his hand. He lights a green flare, its flame immune to the water, and begins walking. We know that it is close and search. I see it first, and Taren lights another flare. I point to the risen rock. Taren gives me the flare and I hold it up as high as I can. He uses the javelin to launch himself onto the rock. The weight of the helmet is only slight beneath the waves. He adjusts himself and turns to lower the javelin to me. I take hold and lift up onto the stone. Now is my time. Now I will make this all worthwhile.

Taren lights another flare and I wipe the sand away from the Fjordooli writing. It clouds. I unzip the pack strapped to my thigh and extra flares fall out. I fumble with them, catching what I can, and rummage around until I find the paper and pencil attached to it with a simple piece of yarn. I pick up the flares and shove them back into my pack before sealing it. In the dark, with the sand being reluctant, sweat beads on my forehead. This takes too long, I know it. Taren says nothing, his eyes searching the darkness always, his grip tight on the javelin. For a moment it looks like his gaze follows something I cannot see. I try not to think of it.

I concentrate on my task, careful to be quick, but also accurate. I know we are not alone down here. In my peripheral a line of glowing dots swirl and dance in the water. It grows close and backs away, its true form always staying out of the light of our flare. I finish my translation and stuff the paper into the pack at my thigh. Taren hands me the flare and holds onto the javelin with both hands. The dots disappear into the darkness.

I drop down off of the rock, pulling the metal helmet against my shoulders. Taren hands me the javelin so he can do the same. I light a flare with the javelin loose in my grip and turn to an open mouth. Teeth long as my fingers greet me and snap just beyond reach. I scream into my helmet. Bulbous black eyes come close, dangling over the mouth from tendrils. I back into Taren who turns. He steals the javelin and jabs it outward towards the teeth. He slices through flesh beyond the jaws and black blood seeps into the light of the flare.

The creature leaves behind a current of water, pressing me back against Taren. He pushes me forward and I take hold of the rope attached to my belt. We pull ourselves back into the glow of the diving bell. Taren boosts me up and Setsui takes hold of my helmet when I break surface. The weight lifts from my shoulders and I grip the edge of the seat. I watch the water, waiting for eyes or teeth, but finding only Taren who comes from below, poking the javelin upward for Setsui to grab. She pulls him up and attaches the weapon to the side of the bell. We strap down the helmets and catch our breath before hoisting ourselves up onto the seat. I need help and Taren grips my belt to lift me out of the water.

"What happened? I heard her scream through the tube," Setsui ticks her head to the metal helmets. The tubes fed into the bell to give us air. "Should I do the bubble?" she asks.

Taren shakes his head and to my surprise, attaches his unlit glass helmet.

"No," the glass muffles his voice, "A creature hunts us. Let me." He withdraws a hunting knife from his belt and Setsui hands him a red inflated ball with a net of wire wrapped around it and excess dangling. He drops down into the water.

I know that right now, as we discussed many times, he climbs up the side of the bell and attaches the ball to the wire that will pull us up. The ball will float to the surface in haste and alert the crew above to pull us up. Our packs are similar to this ball. Should we need it, they will inflate, keeping all of our items inside and bring us up to the surface in an emergency. He came up with these ideas. I admire Taren's mind for a moment. He planned all of this with only ancient and simple tools. Just as most don't think of my mind, I realize I don't think of Taren's. He is smart. He is kind to me. He is kind to his crew.

Seconds turn into minutes. I exchange a glance with Setsui. She nods and grabs her helm when he breaks surface and pulls himself up onto the seat. He takes off the helmet and gasps. The air grows stuffy in here. I know we need to leave soon. Once we break through the bubble of dead, or dead zone as Taren calls it, that protects the stone from technology, our oxygen tanks will function. But first we must do that.

Taren lets the flare in his hand die and cast us into the darkness.

"They eat up oxygen," he offers.

I nod, to myself. Deep, slow breaths. Count to eight.

Samiyah

The bell shifts and we lift upward. I lay my hand on my chest. Thank Parishioner's God. I am ready to be back in our room. On the bed. Reading Parishioner's notes.

Minutes pass and the glow of lights inside the bell come back to life. Taren helps me with my glass helmet and oxygen before seeing to his own. He knows I'm delicate. I hate it.

We all smile at each other. It is done.

Something brushes the bottom of my foot and I look down to a pair of large, black, bulbous eyes floating by my feet. Teeth open up below and I yelp as a thick, black tongue shoots up out of the water and twirls around my leg. It yanks me down into the darkness and I reach out, screaming, as the bell's circular halo of light rapidly grows smaller. Taren yells over the comms at the crew to stop the ascent. I turn to my captor and bend down to detach the pack from my thigh. It loops around my wrist and I tug on the string. It inflates and slows our descent, but not enough to stop.

I cry. Kicking. Screaming. Begging for mercy from Parishioner's God. From Parishioner.

"Please," I sob. "Help."

In the darkness beyond the light of my headlamp bubbles swirl as the javelin flies past. Black blood erupts from the creature below me. The grip on my leg loosens, but remains. We halt. I look up and Taren's headlamp blinds me as he hooks his suit to mine with the belt attachment. The monster recovers and pulls us both down. I fumble with our attachment.

"Just go. Don't die with me," I sob.

He grips my hand, stilling it, "Never."

The lights blink out on our suits. We swim in the dead zone.

I scream. Hear nothing but water rushing past. My oxygen doesn't work. I use my precious air. Raised in the hot sun of the ranch desert, I will die here in the cold dark water. Perhaps this is how it feels to be born. Dark. Wet. I hope to see Parishioner. I hope to see home planet. Maybe in the darkness of death I can be free. At least.

I squeeze my eyes shut, gripping what I can of Taren.

The tongue squeezing my leg shudders. Taren's arm curls around my waist and with a jolt we shoot upward, rising faster than the bell. Our suits come to life. Oxygen blows into my helmet. I breathe deep, gasping. Taren looks up, holding onto his flotation device, his arm around my waist. My own flotation tugs my wrist upward and together we fly past the bell.

"Raise the bell," he says over the comms.

We bump against the sheet of ice covering the surface, the blessed white light shines through thinner spots. Taren kicks his feet and I join him as we make our way to the circular opening. I spot the red ball bobbing in the waves when we break surface.

We detach and I reach up. Firm hands hoist me out of the water. I collapse to my knees on the ice and slide around. The water clings to me, freezing. I crawl stiffly away from the opening.

Over the comms Taren says, "Get Setsui up and leave the damn bell."

He rises out of the ocean and brushes off a thin layer of freezing water from his suit. The pirate detaches his flotation device and discards it, but I keep hold of mine. It has our precious translation. He kneels next to me and slowly removes the tongue still gripping my leg. As he does, I suck in my breath. Suckers pop and rip holes in my suit and skin.

"Shit," he tosses the tongue he cut in the darkness to save me.

The wounds puff and Taren grips my hands to hoist me to my feet. He wraps his arms around my shoulder and behind my knees to lift me. I curl up in his grasp. The biting cold stings on the fresh wounds and my own blood seeping from them freezes on contact. My oxygen works overtime with the leak in my suit. My teeth chatter as he presses on in the howling wind. Up the slope of the coast to the gaping mouth of the shuttle.

"Get your asses in here," he huffs over the comms. "We need to leave."

The crew are close behind us. Setsui is safe out of the water and they bark at each other to gather up only necessary equipment. We leave the massive diving bell behind. I imagine it sinking down to the desolate bottom once the wire gives way to decades of neglect. Our presence here will erase soon enough.

Taren sets me down on the seat and reaches into an overhead compartment, withdrawing a first aid kit. He opens it and rummages, finding a medicinal bandage. He rips open the packaging and wraps it around the wounds on my leg. I suck in my breath. He ties it off and tosses the kit back into the compartment, shutting it.

He buckles me in and sits in the pilot's chair and the engine whirs to life beneath us. The crew scramble in, strapping down cases of equipment before themselves. They confirm headcount. The door shuts and air hisses as the cabin cycles out the methane to fill with oxygen. They remove their helmets and wipe down their faces.

I leave mine on. I don't want to move. When I blink I see the eyes. Feel the tongue. My leg stings as pain climbs up to my thigh.

4. Samiyah

In the white sterile infirmary I trace my fingertips over the fresh circular scars on my leg. Tears stream down my face. Setsui tries to console me, but there is none. I have flaws. I am worthless. They fade when she treats me, but in the light their shiny surface glistens. Three perfect rows from my mid-calf down to my ankle. It almost looks intentional. A tattoo gift from the monster under the waves.

"I'll take you to the room," she says.

I don't want to go there. Taren will find me. Find me flawed and worthless. Perhaps his disgust of me will finally be the last straw. He will give me back to Varashka. Who will be angry with my scars. Who will punish me. I know it. And then what I don't know. Don't want to.

But I follow her down the halls in a long white tunic and loose pants. Similar to my loungewear on the ranch. After we reached the dock of Whydah, Taren was called to the bridge. We went into hyperspace immediately after. Now we float next to a colorful nebula. It takes up the whole of the view window in the room.   Setsui leaves me in peace. I pick up Parishioner's bag in the corner and stuff my things into it. I will depart soon. I know it.

The door hisses open behind me.

"What are you doing?" Taren walks over to his dresser and digs clothes out. His wetsuit is still on.

"Packing," I say in the smallest voice I can.

He unzips the front of his suit and withdraws his arms. He pulls a black tunic over his bare torso. I force myself to look down and away. I turn my back to him, and as we have done many times before, I know he changes into his other pants. The suit crumples next to him on the floor when I face him.

"You're not going anywhere," he says. "Put your things away."

I shake my head, frowning. "I'm not?"

"No. Why would you?"

I inhale and open my mouth, but rather than words, I lift up the leg of my pants and point to the scars.

His black gaze follows my movement.

"It won't happen again."

He doesn't know my meaning.

"No..." I straighten. "I disgust you now. You don't have to be nice about it. I can leave your sight. Perhaps, I can stay in Parishioner's old—"

"What's the matter with you?" he asks. His confusion baffles me.

"What?"

"You want to leave because you think you disgust me?"

I blink, "Don't I?"

"I thought you wanted to leave because of the danger."

I shake my head, "No. No. Never."

"You don't disgust me," he takes a step forward. "Scars mean nothing. I have many."

I know he does, but I am different.

My brows furrow, "No. You are still many things. I am not. This is it. This is me. This is all I am meant to be. All I am good for. Beauty. With these, I am not beauty. I am not myself. Not what I am meant to be. I am nothing." My lips tremble. Tears spill onto my cheeks. "Nothing."

"No," his voice rises. His hands clench into fists.

I back away.

"That's bullshit." He takes a step towards me. I press back against the cool metal wall and he cages me between his arms. "Get that foolishness out of your head. Now."

"But I—"

"Now!" His fist slams against the wall beside me. I jump.

I nod. Not because I understand. My breath is shallow and I part my lips.

"You are not nothing, Samiyah."

I swallow. My eyes widen as he draws near.

His voice lowers, "Say it."

"I am not nothing," I tremble.

"You are...everything." He leans in, pressing his lips to mine. He lowers his hands to take hold of my wrists, drawing them up over my head. He pins them to the wall and his warm body presses against mine.

Our lips part. I am breathless.

"You think I keep you here, with me," his lips ghost against mine, "just because you are pretty?"

"Yes," I say. This is true. "It's the only reason everyone keeps me. Except—"

"Me."

I was going to say Parishioner.

I inhale a shuddering breath. I know what I want from Taren cannot be. My lady always told me it isn't possible. Not for me.

"Of course," I lick my lips and glance down at his. "You need me to read Fjordooli."

Taren releases me and sits on the edge of the bed. He runs his hand down his face and it lingers over his mouth. His penetrating dark gaze watches me.

I lean against the wall. My legs are weak.

"I do," he finally says. "But it's more than that."

I knew it. I slide down to the floor and hug my knees.

He pats the bed next to him, "I'm sorry I touched you. I didn't ask."

I crawl up to the bed and climb on. Our thighs touch, as they have so many times.

His voice is soft, "I think there's something you should know."

He starts and stops himself many times. I take his hand in mine and turn to face him, tucking my leg beneath me. I stroke his hand like Parishioner might do.

"It is okay," I say. "You can tell me anything." Parishioner's words, but I do mean them.

"Sylvester was right about me. I can be false. Sometimes it's necessary, but sometimes it's not. But believe me, I am not being false now. I am not being false with you," he looks down at our grasp. "You're smart."

My mind? My lips tremble.

"You're kind."

My soul? I squeeze his hand and he presses mine.

"Do you really think I risked my life to save you because you're pretty?" His dark eyes snap up to mine.

Do I?

I can't answer, he continues.

"There are ranches like Cademe's all over the galaxy cluster. I can find a dozen pretty girls. I can find women with ethereal beauty beyond yours. I can even find other scholars who speak Fjordooli. I can—"

I slap him. How dare he give me hope. How dare he. I almost believe. My chest heaves with the air I cannot get enough of. He holds his red cheek. I pull my hand back again, but he catches my wrist. He pins my arms behind me, pressing our chests together. His eyes gleam. I only pretend to struggle in his grasp, but I arch my back and tip my chin upward to him. He fists my hair, holding me in place, and lowers his lips to mine. I open my mouth and moan.

He crushes me in his grip. I slide into his lap and wrap my arms around his neck. I yank the bottom of his tunic over his head, rustling his hair. My hands roam the dips and grooves of his chest and stomach as I have desired to so many times. He tugs my hips down, grinding us together in mock of what we wish for. I gasp when his hands slide down my back past the hem of my pants. He kneads the flesh of my backside and a blush coats my face and neck while I slide my hand down between his legs. He moans and breaks our kiss.

Taren rips the collar of my tunic and his hot mouth sucks on my neck, shoulders, ears. Then he tears it off of me completely. He latches onto my hardened nipple and I card my hands into his thick hair. I throw my head back in a silent scream. With each stroke of his tongue and hands the moisture between my legs increases. The folds are slick and I'm anxious for him to fill me. So I can be complete. Fulfill my purpose.

Samiyah

He turns, and flips me around onto my back. I smile as he slides the waist of my pants down my hips. I curl my legs up and he smiles as he grasps my ankles and parts my thighs. I let him, biting my finger, keeping his stare. His deft hand cups me and his fingers dip into wet heat. I arch my back, moaning, clawing the sheets.

Nothing like this. Never did I think it possible. So many times my lady trained me to pretend to enjoy this. To act. Be false. Convincing. When he leans down and sucks on my nub, I fist his hair and my toes curl. This is not an act. This isn't false.

I know he's experienced. He is too good at this. I don't care. The muscles between my legs tighten involuntarily. I bite my lip and whine. He curls his fingers inside of me and my muscles seize before releasing into waves of bliss. I cry out and grip his hair.

I lay back, panting.

He unbuttons his pants. His girth penetrates me. At first, pain. I know to expect it, but lining it is bliss. Pleasure. Want. I desire more. His lips press to my neck and he stills. I draw my knees up on either side of him, and with each wave of discomfort I claw against the skin of his back. My brows furrow and I moan, in the contrast of agony and elation. He curls his arms around me and withdraws only to snap back. I yelp with the movement. My breasts bounce and his mouth catches my hard nipple.

Again he moves within me. And again. And again, until we move together. Until the pain is a dull ache and fire ignites in my gut. The butterflies dance in the heat of our joining bodies. I want this to never end. I hook my ankles behind him and he listens to my body. Driving me into the mattress, hooking his hands on my shoulders to keep me against him.

Too soon the end nears. I tighten around his width. He moans and swears, his breath hot and steamy on my neck. I dig my nails into his back and tilt my head, exposing my neck to him as deep from within a wail escapes my lips while I contract. Waves of satisfaction pulse through my body as he finishes inside me.

We pant together. He rests on his elbows, even now, careful to keep from crushing me beneath his weight. Sweat coats our skin.

This isn't false. At least, not for me.

I sleep so well and when I wake it is in his embrace.

I snuggle into his neck under the sheets. In his sleep he pulls me close.

I don't want to wake him, so I still in thought. I wonder if Varashka will still want me. I am fine with this if he doesn't. I don't want him too.

The screen on the desk rises and chimes with an incoming message from the bridge. Taren stirs and sits up, untangling from me. He blinks with sleep and rubs his eyes. The screen blips on and Dennon's red face fills it.

"Oh," he averts his eyes.

Though I have the sheet up to my shoulders, it is obvious what we have done. Taren glances at me and offers a crooked smile, leaning over to put himself between me and the screen.

"What is it Dennon?"

Behind him, I slide my hands up his back and over his shoulders, down his chest and abs. The sheet falls as I do and I press my breasts against his warm back. I cannot help myself. I want to join with him again.

I kiss the nape of his neck.

"A ship is requesting to dock."

Taren takes my hand from his abdomen and kisses the palm.

"Who?"

"Lady Cademe."

My hand stills and he grips the other.

"What?"

Dennon nods, "Cademe."

"All right," Taren glances over his shoulder to me. "Let her in."

I swallow and my heart quickens. Why is my lady here? I thought to never see her again. I lay my cheek against Taren's back. He holds my hand, kissing the palm, lingering it over his mouth. We sit in silence for a moment as the screen blackens and lowers down.

We both know she is here for me. We dress and I borrow Taren's shirt, as mine is laying in a ripped crumple. We both laugh and smile, helping each other fasten buttons, stealing a kiss or caress. But we somber as we walk through the halls. Taren arms himself, which is unusual when we are on Whydah.

"Will she take me?" I ask, though I know the answer.

Taren shakes his head, "I won't let her."

"I don't think it's your decision." My lady's tendrils reach into the outer edges of the cluster and beyond. She knows everyone, everywhere. And everyone knows her. There is a reason one such as Varashka won't cross her. She has people to find us. To dispense her punishment. I think my pirate knows this as well as I.

His brows furrow. I know this look. I witnessed it over the years on the ranch, when buyers were forced to part with me. But this time I mirror the feeling. I don't want to go. I don't want to part with Taren. Tears well my eyes and I wipe my cheeks. He takes my hand in his and interlaces our fingers. He squeezes.

"At least," my breath catches. "At least we…" I can't finish. I think he knows what I want to say.

"I'll think of something," he says as we near the door to the dock.

It hisses open and Taren releases my hand to put his over the hilt of his pistol. My lady waits, with the patience she always possesses. Stock surround her that I recognize. Not old friends, but familiar faces. Enforcers. Protectors. They serve her. They are dangerous.

My lady lifts her light brows and smiles, rising from the wicker chair set out by the stock. She offers both of her hands to Taren, forcing him to release his grip on the pistol handle. He takes them and leans in for her to kiss both of his pale cheeks.

"No need for that Taren," she glances at his pistol and behind to those of his crew who hold onto their guns.

I did not know they are acquainted.

He swallows and releases her, taking a step closer to me.

"You know I come to fetch Samiyah," though pleasant, my lady is always straightforward. "You have tortured poor Varashka long enough. It is time he gets his merchandise back."

I swallow and step forward when she beckons.

Taren blocks my path and replaces his hand on his pistol, "And I suppose you have come to fetch her for him? Can't he do it his damn self?"

My lady raises her brows and smiles, glancing down at his weapon, "We both know that's a bad idea."

"What will it take to keep her?" Taren asks.

I close my fingers around his hand. In my lady's presence I don't want to cry. The sadness is a deep well within.

My butterflies die as I say, "It is all right. Let me go."

My lady's silver eyes flicker to our grasp. Taren won't release me and she raises her gaze to mine.

"A contract is a contract, Mr. Valannon. You of all people know this."

Taren's last name. I forget that others have them. Stock like me do not. I wonder if Parishioner has one. Had one.

I try to slip from his grip, but he doesn't let go. His hand sweats. He swallows. Scowls. I fear he's going to do something foolish.

Silence hangs heavy. Taren won't release me, my lady won't leave without me. The butterflies in my stomach thrash. My lady and pirate stare at each other. The crew grip their guns. The stock around my lady draw theirs, fast, like lightning to take aim. Taren's crew return the favor and I find myself the only one without a weapon training on me. I yank from Taren, his grip is a vice.

"Please! You must let me go! I can't let you do this!" I cry.

He remains, still, not giving me up. Then I feel it. The cold metal of a gun barrel against my head. I didn't see or hear the stock walk up. Neither did Taren. He concentrates on my lady. The gun whirs to life by my temple and I still. Panting.

"No one steals from me or my clients," my lady's voice is cold. I know this tone. She means what she says. "You won't have her either way."

Sweat pours down my neck and my hand trembles in Taren's.

"Oh yeah? And who exactly is going to enforce it?" my pirate asks. I don't know his meaning. My lady has people who do these things for her.

"Keep in mind I retain half my pay if she dies. It's no skin off my back. Let her go," my lady says. "Please."

What she says hurts me, and I wonder if she lies. Or maybe I seek something from her that was never there.

Taren glances to the gun against my head and releases me.

"I like you, Taren," she raises her hand and flicks it forward. Two stock, large, muscular, approach him. "But I can't make an exception. Even for you. Give up the gun. Give up the girl."

Taren relinquishes his pistol. His crew keep their weapons on my lady and her stock who strike the pirate in his jaw. Taren falls without a fight. His crew lurch forward, but he waves them back. They still, watching with wide eyes. Setsui growls. I lurch forward, but the stock grabs my arm, keeping me up. I thrash against him as his partners kick Taren. Their fists collide with his body. Their feet make contact with his ribs.

"Please!" I scream. I pull and yank. Driving my elbows into the ribs of the stock, I force him to release me with a groan. I dive to Taren, shielding him with my body from their flying fists and feet.

"Don't touch her," my lady says. They stop and stand back, panting. They already know not to touch me.

I hover my hands over him, unsure of where I can place them. Taren shudders and cracks open his eye. His crew close in, their guns ready. Setsui has hers on my lady.

"Just give the word boss," she says taking aim.

Taren shakes his head and waves his hand. Bruises well on his face and blood runs from his mouth. He sits up, I help him. I trace my fingers along his jaw. I am so angry.

I turn on my lady, "Leave him be. Please. Just take me. But don't touch him." Tears fall from my eyes. "Please don't hurt him anymore."

My lady scowls. She hates crying. I do so much of it now, but I don't care. I walk to her and Taren grabs my tunic, but his grip is weak and I pull away. I lean down and kiss the palm of his hand.

"I'm so sorry," I whisper to him.

"No," his voice is weak. He reaches out again, but it's too easy to break away. "No," he crawls towards me.

My lady reaches for me and I take her hand.

"I hate you," I whisper.

To my surprise, her brows furrow. She isn't angry. Maybe sad? She is gentle with me as we turn. Her hand rests on the small of my back. I glance over my shoulder and stop. I memorize Taren's features. I will never see him again. I know it. His thick brown hair. His paper white skin. I see past the bruises and blood to the man I know is beneath. He risks everything for me. He isn't false.

"Captain?" Setsui asks, daring a step closer with her drawn weapon. When she does, the stock train all of their guns on her captain.

"I'll double what he paid," my pirate coughs and lifts himself from the floor. He staggers. "All contracts have loopholes."

My lady smiles. This time it goes to her eyes. Then she laughs, my hand shaking in her grasp. The stock chuckle with her. This isn't funny to me. It makes me sorry for my pirate. It's impossible. I appreciate his efforts, but I want to leave without his death. He isn't already a corpse, I know, as a favor to him and me.

"It's okay," I say again. "Let me go. Please."

"Never," he wipes the blood on his chin, smearing it. He settles his weight on one leg and pushes his hair out of his face. I think this may not be the first time he experiences this kind of pain.

My lady recovers with a deep breath and stifles her laughter, "I might entertain the idea if you actually have the money."

Now Taren smiles, cocking his head to the side. "You think I don't?"

My lady's smile disappears.

"I do," he shrugs. Casual, but his gaze is hard. Jaw tight.

"You," she looks him up and down, taking in his disheveled appearance, "have twelve million speks?"

Taren's eyes lock onto mine. My lips part. I can't get enough breath. I am not worth that. No one is.

"Closer to thirteen if you want to get technical."

My lady waves her hand and the stock lower their guns, but she keeps hold of me.

"Even if you do have it, she isn't worth such a price."

The pirates keep their guns on my lady and her stock. Taren doesn't tell them to do otherwise.

"I think you already know she is. To me. I let your flunkies do what they did to prove how serious I am. You need to understand that if you don't sell her to me," he raises his fist and the crew close in with their weapons drawn. "I'm willing to risk your wrath.

And if you kill her, you risk mine. And it will not be easy for you. Or quick. Or painless."

My lady holds her head high as she calculates. She measures. I know this look. I do not know what Taren is capable of, but I know what my lady can do. Her grey eyes dart to Taren and his crew and land only once on me.

She smiles and a stock hands her the tablet I have seen her conduct so many sales on. Including my own. She offers it to Taren.

"Well, Mr. Valannon. If you really do have the money, show me. Then I am open to ideas."

Taren is stiff as he draws close. He keeps his eyes on my lady and takes the tablet from her. He wipes his bloody hand on his tunic before the tablet chimes and beeps for him to input his information.

"I'm not—"

He cuts me off, "You are." He glances at me with a quick smile that dies when his black eyes refocus on the screen.

He returns the tablet to my lady and she keeps her face neutral.

"Excellent," she runs her fingers over the tablet. "Twelve million speks for Samiyah. She isn't yours until the transfer is complete and the transfer cannot be complete until the contract with Varashka is violated or void. So," she lets me go and gestures to the two of us. "I need you to be honest about something."

I raise my eyebrows and Taren wastes no time in taking my hand and tugging me to him.

My lady's eyes dance down to our entangled clasp and back up with a smile, "You have taken her purity."

Taren narrows his eyes.

"It's perfect," my lady claps her hands together. "Varashka's contract is null and void due to a violation of terms from my side of the bargain. He paid for her in full, including her virtue. Her virtue cannot be delivered and now the contract is no more. I refund his money with a five hundred spek fine and we are done. You did lose your purity, right?"

She looks at me.

I open my mouth, but can't bring myself to say the words.

"Samiyah, this is important. Did Varashka take your purity, or did this man?"

I sidle close to Taren and clutch him. He's warm. His arm wraps around me.

"He did."

"He who, dear?" she grows impatient.

"Taren," I whisper.

"Perfect. Mr. Valannon. If you will," she offers him the tablet.

Taren places the whole of his hand on it and a line of light scans down.

"I'm sure you understand she comes in an 'as is' condition," her pupils dilate as the money transfers to her account. She is quite happy.

"Don't we all?" he asks.

Guilt weighs down my elation. How many years did the man in black work to get this money? How hard? How many other things did he do without to save it? Did his fingers bleed for it? Did the crew's? Even my lady does not have such money. Until now.

The scan finishes and Taren lowers his hand.

"Excellent," a stock takes the device from my lady. "A pleasure Taren. As always." She gestures to me, "She is all yours. I will notify Varashka of the contract termination immediately. He won't bother you anymore."

Samiyah

"Good," Taren lets go of my hand to put his arm around my shoulders. I am his now. My heart leaps. "Now get the fuck off my ship."

Taren sits on the cold table where Parishioner died in the white infirmary. He doesn't release my hand. I stand next to him as Setsui tends his wounds. The small pen she grips whirs and chimes. He doesn't flinch as she goes over his bruises and cuts.

"Why'd you let them do it?" she asks hovering the pen over a welt on his cheek.

He smiles and watches my reaction instead of hers, "Lady Cademe won't kill me. You know that. We do too much business together. I just want her to realize how serious I am. I let them beat me because I can. Now she can imagine what I'll do if I'm actually upset. Motivated."

My brows furrow, "She could have killed you."

"A gamble I was willing to make."

"You do stock business with her?" I ask, ready to be disappointed.

He shakes his head, "No. Other business."

"Who do you think tracks down the people who piss her off?" Setsui chuckles to herself, running the healing pen over Taren's bloody mouth. "There's good money in it."

"She attributed to a lot of my savings," he laughs with his second in command.

I do not join them, "I am not worth that much money. You shouldn't have done it."

He brings my hand to his lips, the pen moving down to his collar bone.

"You are to me."

I blush under his hot gaze and reward him with a smile. Setsui rewards him with a gagging noise.

She grunts and Taren releases me to pull the tunic over his head. Dark bruises blotch his torso. Blood oozes from welts and cuts. I gasp. This is awful.

Setsui glances up from her work, "Don't feel too bad. When we get the replicator he'll make that twelve million back and then some."

"Replicator?" I ask.

They exchange a glance.

"Yes," Taren sucks in a breath as Setsui continues down to his chest. "You didn't know?"

I shake my head and shrug, "Know what?"

"That's what we're looking for. I thought Sylvester told you."

"No," the memory of him pains me, "No. I just want to help."

Taren smiles.

"So see?" Setsui traces the pen over a bruise and it melts away to healthy skin. "Don't feel bad. Taren will make more than his money back once we get it."

I know she tries to comfort me with this, but instead I wonder if he is false. He glares at her and she focuses on the pen.

He bought me for Fjordooli then?

I do like the thought of being purchased for my mind instead of my body, but I hope he bought me for the other reason. The big reason. The one my lady says is impossible for me. I hop up and sit on the table next to him.

"That's not why I bought you," he takes my hand. A brief, silly fear he can read minds flashes. He winces when Setsui reaches his ribs, "And I'll file for your freedom papers when we port next. I promise."

I smile, but still wonder.

Samiyah

On the walk back to our room, Taren tells me the Fjordooli were an ancient race of aliens who explored far beyond the galaxy cluster. Past the border of dark matter. Their technology was advanced and any artifacts left behind are worth tens of millions of speks on the black market. The replicator is mentioned only a few times in their histories, but Taren found the first clue by accident. He hired a translator before he convinced Parishioner to join him, but they quit, feeling it too dangerous. Thinking of my new scars, I understand. The replicator is the only one of its kind and can replicate anything in the universe that is carbon based. Taren says this can help to make a lot of money. And honestly. Or at least no violence. So long as the Cluster Artifact Authority doesn't find out we possess it. They take all of the Fjordooli possessions. I never knew who these ancient aliens were, nor did I care. I learned Fjordooli because Parishioner talked of it all the time. It was a way for us to spend time together. And when not together, it was something to think about other than the fate waiting for me.

I wonder aloud, "Can we replicate Parishioner?"

He holds my hand as we walk, "No. We would just copy his corpse. There is no cloning of souls I'm afraid. I think we can clone someone alive, but not someone who's entirely dead. But then again, I don't really know how it all works. So I guess we can be mad scientists and experiment."

"Angry scientists?" I ask.

"No, insane. Mad means insane."

"Like Varashka," I watch my feet as we walk.

"Yes, like him." He squeezes my hand, "He won't bother us anymore."

The door to our room hisses open. We detach and Taren kicks off his boots before sitting on the bed at his desk. He pulls up the screen and loads the picture he took of my writing from under the ocean and studies it.

I bite my lip and watch, sliding onto the bed behind him. I want to join with him again, but I don't know how to tell him so.

"If the Fjordooli are so advanced, why can't we have technology around them?"

"That's a part of their technology. Those stones have some kind of EMP affect at all times. Instead of a pulse, it's a steady stream. They kill technology. And I suppose those are worth money by themselves, but good luck getting that thing on a ship. It would be impossible to break down and reverse engineer without technology."

He focuses on the screen and I tug my clothes off. I lay naked behind him, my back against the wall with my legs tucked up. I raise my hands over my head in a manner I was taught to lift my breasts.

"And that is why you bought me," I'm so sure. "Because I will make you more money than you spent."

"I will, but Samiyah, how many times do I have to tell you that's not wh—" Taren turns and rests his eyes on me.

His crooks a smile, the screen forgotten, as he turns to crawl over me. I giggle as he grips my hips and yanks me until I slide beneath him. Our mouths lock and I roll him over onto his back. I want to show him my training. I want him to feel he will get his money's worth. At least some. I unbutton his pants and take his heavy flesh in my hand before wrapping my lips around it. So warm. Salty. His fingers card into my hair and he moans beneath me, bucking his hips. He swears when I pull away, and pants, but he is not done. I am selfish.

He sits up, me in his lap. With his hand guiding my hip we join and for a moment pain supersedes fulfillment. I know to expect pain the second time, but I forgot. It is not as bad as the first and in a moment I'm moving over him. With him. My hands card into his hair and his chin tips to steal a kiss as I rise and lower. His hands grip my hips.

This is slow. Not as frantic. Our panting fills the cabin. This is not false.

Seventeen cycles later we arrive at the next destination.

The planet below is red and brown. A desert planet. Not like the desert of the ranch or home planet. Worse. A continual storm blows sand and dirt and clay. Winds so high we have to plan around them. Taren says the dirt is so thick the light of the suns is weak on the surface. I ask if this will be dangerous and they all assure me it isn't. At least, not as dangerous as the ocean.

I wear Taren's clothes beneath my spacesuit. I do not have many of my own. I prefer his. They are worn and soft. Smell like him. We roll up the pants and I borrow a crewmember's shoes. I like this look. I'm not so...beautiful. I braid my hair almost always instead of letting it flow as taught. Taren says nothing of my new look. I think he likes it, but maybe he doesn't say anything because he doesn't. He still joins with me many times a day. I'm hopeful. I think there may be that thing between us my lady says is impossible for me.

The shuttle on our descent shudders and I squeeze my eyes shut. I'm thankful I can't see outside and that Taren pilots. I trust him with my life. As does the crew we travel with. Though I cannot see, I know we push through the high wind towards the settlement below. This is the open window, according to the weather report, where we can fly in moderate safety. An entirely subjective word at this moment. We need to reach their dock and get inside the protective dome, then below. Then we will really be safe.

I open my eyes to stare at the back of the captain's chair. I can never see Taren as he pilots. I make the mistake of glancing past to the viewer and lines of green outlining obstacles and landing ways that would otherwise not be seen past the thick curtain of dust and dirt. I close my eyes again and cover my ears. I will go in darkness as I came from darkness. Please. Please let the computers be true with their guidance. I do not need to wish for Taren's steady hand.

But the shuttle jolts down in a torrent of wind before lurching back up. I yelp and an arm reaches around my shoulder. I peek to Setsui. Her eyes close too, but she relaxes, almost napping in her seat. I lean into her and she holds me close.

Another drop, another panic in my chest, and then we straighten. Then a shudder. And finally smooth sailing. I open my eyes and we are inside the calm dome of the dock. Dust and dirt push against the clear glass surface before Taren's chair. There are shuttles like ours flying past and Setsui releases me.

After landing and checking in with the dock master, we go down into the tunnels below. The city beneath the surface. Lively. Bright neon lights. So many people, aliens, others. Despite the inhospitable atmosphere above, the population thrives. I have never been to such a place. So many shops and windows with displays. Some of the displays are stock like me. Or like I once was. Dancing and showing off their assets. But they reveal more than I was ever allowed to. I wonder if they are happy working in such a bright and beautiful place.

Machine music blares from store doors into a distorted, fun symphony. Little cafes with tables dot the long and wide walkway. The food smells delicious. Trays bear neon drinks that glow in the lights of the walkway. So many different aliens, others, and even a few pure humans like me. Or mostly pure.

I hover close to Taren, but can't help watching everyone around us with wonder. I want to enter each little store and see what wares they have to offer. Instead, we walk to the end of the lively thoroughfare. Shops become less frequent and the walkway descends down. Now there are streets with small vehicles and cycles. The dip in the ground allows for a taller ceiling with buildings stacking up to the maximum height. Many of their windows are lit with a soft yellow glow. These are homes now. And there are shops, but not the same kind. These sell everyday items. Humble. Less glamorous. No shining neon lights. Plain signs hang in the light of the streetlamps. It is sleepy. Stuck in eternal night under the ground.

I do not pay attention as we navigate because I don't need to. We follow Taren, who walks the roads down to a crowded train station. The trains run along old railways. Taren buys tickets from a robot at the booth and our crew pile into a passenger car. It is clean. Well maintained, but old. Used. We stop and switch trains at many stations. Out the windows are rough, uneven ground and the occasional mosaics of stone. The scenery flies by so fast I can only glimpse a palette of dull color. The further we travel the worse the rails. The less glamorous the stops. The fewer the people.

Finally, we shudder to a stop at our destination and Taren stands with his pack. I shoulder mine and follow with the crew. The station, below ground as they all are, is constructed of expensive material. Marble floors, but a layer of dust coats them. Columns of the same marble dot the landing with scenes depicting beautiful landscapes. Some squares of the mosaic are missing.

We approach the booth manned by a single red alien who reads a tablet.

Taren places his hand over the scanner next to the window and the alien comes to attention, lowering their tablet. The pirate looks over the admissions prices and other listed items.

"Three thousand tokens please," he says, keeping his hand on the scanner. I watch as the numbers empty out of his bank account.

"That will be three thousand speks. No refunds or exchanges. All purchases final," the alien reaches down with an extra set of arms and produces three rolls of tokens wrapped in parchment. Taren takes them and the alien gets back to their tablet. We move on.

This is a ghost town. I do not know why we are here, but I follow Taren through the tunnel opening up to a small round community. Closed shops line a neat circle around a solitary, large building. The cavern is high and stalactites that were so carefully cut down to a smooth surface in the big city, hang neglected and low here. Water drips from their tips to the marble floor beneath us.

This place can be beautiful cleaned up. Instead it is abandoned. There are no electrical lights either. Torches and gas lamps illuminate us. Thousands. The smoke rolls up into a vent in the ceiling, keeping the air clear.

"Hungry?" Taren asks.

A few of the crewmembers nod and we shuffle to the only open shop in the circle. The door opens to steam and aroma of sizzling meat. The counter is clean. The dessert display glass shines. I smile when the clerk bows and greets us. She is mostly human. She seems happy to have so many of us. We pay for our meals with tokens. When Taren and I sit alone, I laugh when I notice the cooling rocks in the drink are miniature versions of Fjordooli stones.
Taren smiles at me.

"What is this place?" I ask.

He swallows a mouthful, "This is a tourist trap. Or it used to be."

"Trap?" My eyes dart around, searching for danger.

"No," he laughs and shakes his head. "Not like that. This is a Fjordooli stone that's well known. For centuries people flocked here to look at it. It helped build Disca. That was the city we came through. Anyway, the thing is, this stone isn't like the others. Fjordooli scholars studied it for years, but there isn't any Fjordooli actually on it. It was declared a fake, even though technology can't work around it, like it should. I think their egos were hurt. The last clue leads us here. So...I think it's real after all. We should try. Otherwise it's a dead end."

He doesn't seem hopeful as he takes a drink.

It is up to me. I know it is. I will try. I take his hand in mine and gaze into his black eyes, "I can do this. For you. I will figure it out." If I don't, he will have bought me for nothing.

"Samiyah, it's okay if you don't." He squeezes and releases me. He eats.

I lose my appetite and only eat at his insistence. I worry. And wonder if the paper and pad in my bag are useless. This place has no danger from the outside, but I feel it from within. Is this where my journey with him ends? I must help him. As he helps me. I must return it. As my lady always says, I must give him something for his money. Nothing is free.

After our meal, we approach the center building and at the door is a ticket booth. An orange tentacle other greets us, waving its tendrils politely. I think politely. It counts us.

"Eight beings. That is 800 tokens please..." It studies Taren, "Sir?"

Taren hands over the tokens and all I can see is more money disappearing from his coffers. The crew mumble they will pay him back. After all, they are promised a fair portion of the replicator money. I am as well, but I don't want any. I just want Taren.

Past the small entryway opens up a large circular room. Torches sputter on the walls between infographics on the Fjordooli. Shadows dance. At the end is a waterfall cascading down to the stone with bench seating before it. The water navigates in a circle carved around the rock to keep the stone itself dry. It creates a ring of glistening waves around it.

I walk up to it. This is my moment. My heart sinks in despair. My brows furrow and I'm careful to keep fear from my face. I can't read it. At all. There is no hint of Fjordooli on it, as Taren said. I set my pack down and dig out my paper and pencil anyway. I am determined.

But hours pass and I have nothing. No one else comes, no other "tourists", but some of the crew leave to look around the compound in their boredom. I know I'm taking too long. And I am not the only one studying it. Taren and Setsui both do as I do, walking around the stone and looking at it from every angle to understand the simple dots and lines that are etched into its surface.

Tears spring to my eyes when Taren sighs and sits down on the bench. I disappoint him. I cannot have that. I cannot have this flaw too. I swallow.

"I will get it," I keep my voice steady. He has invested too much into me.

"It's okay," he says.

My back is to him. My tears fall. I crawl onto the stone, over the duct of water, passing the "do not touch" sign in common. I wipe my eyes and run my fingers along the lines and dots. I hum a tune Parishioner did when I worried. A hymn. It always makes me feel better, but it doesn't work now.

"Samiyah," Taren tires. "Let's go. There's nothing for us here."

I keep humming, following the spiral of symbols.

"Samiyah," his voice is firm. "Let's go. There's nothing we can do."

I shake my head and hum, following the rhythm of the song. The song.

I still, holding my breath. Tears clear my eyes and I follow the trail of symbols. It is a song.

"Samiyah!" Taren reaches over the small duct of water and grabs my arm.

I fling him off. My fingers trail the music. I follow the tunes, humming the song.

"It's okay," his voice is soft. His hand is gentle on my shoulder, but his eyes follow my movements. He quiets, stills, letting me work.

I hum the tune, increasing in volume. I stumble less over the rhythm and tone. Finally, I raise my voice, with no words, only song, and sing it all the way through. I am trained for this.

The stone shudders and jolts. I back into Taren's grasp and he hauls me off of the stone as the sides shift outward, creating a crack down the middle. At the edge we lean over and Taren squeezes me in his arms. He's excited. I smile. I have done what I came to do. I make him happy.

The water from the fall above spills into a small cavern below and disappears down into the darkness. We wait. The water level rises and with it, a simple wooden bowl. Resting on a bundle of cotton within it, is a small, simple thing. A metal circular band. A ring.

The bowl floats forward to the edge near us and Taren reaches out for it, then snatches his hand back.

"You do it Samiyah. I think you've earned it." He puts his arm around my shoulders.

"You don't think it's dangerous?" Setsui asks.

He shakes his head, "If I did for a second I wouldn't let her touch it, but the Fjordooli weren't a violent race. We know this. All of their artifacts benefit life, not impair it."

I reach out and take hold of the bowl. It is small and light. The wood is smooth and polished. I offer it to him.

"Is this it?" I ask as he takes the band.

He swallows, "I think so."

I expect him to pull on the ring, but instead he hides it in a pocket within his jacket. He grabs my hand and we pick up our gear, Setsui hollering for the others. We leave, quickly. The journey back is longer than the journey to. I am anxious to see what it does. But it is not safe to experiment here. Someone may be watching. We cannot get caught with it, or we cannot keep it. We try to be casual as we hurry along our path. From the stations to the undercity, back to the shining beauty of the metropolis. Disca I think he calls it. I want to linger and watch the pretty signs and dancing stock. People laugh and sing and drink and dance together. I want to join them, but we hurry through to the dock and board our shuttle.

We finally have the replicator.

5. Samiyah

Taren gathers the entire crew of the ship in the cargo bay. Hundreds of aliens and humans and others crowd into it. I realize how many there are. More than I expect.

Taren stands on a box and first thanks them. He couldn't do it without them. Any of them. Blood rushes to my cheeks when he kneels on the box and reaches out to me. He thanks me, especially. The crew clap and cheer when I accept his hand and stand on the box with him. Setsui beats her fist against her chest and grins up at me. They all have worked hard on this. I have done nothing, but I don't contradict him in front of his companions.

And now the moment of truth. Taren wants us all to see how this thing works, together. I climb down from the box for safety, at my pirate captain's insistence. There is a wide berth around him as he slides the ring over his finger.

It adjusts to his size instantly. Then it grows, expanding metal along his finger, hand and wrist up to his elbow, stopping at his shoulder. He holds his arm out as it locks into place, covering it in a smooth glove of shining metal. A panel rises up from the surface at the top of his forearm and he holds out his palm to us, revealing a shining, swirling rainbow of color. It appears like a doorway to another dimension.

We all gasp at the beauty of colors in his palm.

"Does it hurt?" I ask over the shouts of confusion and joy.

He shakes his head with a smile.

Then the panel finalizes and I recognize the Fjordooli symbols projecting upwards from it. Taren sits on the edge of the box and leans down to me.

"Main menu," I say. Then I point to each corresponding button, translating.

It seems I may need to teach my pirate Fjordooli after all.

Taren and I join many times tonight. We hardly sleep. And at the start of the next cycle, he gives me a small chip. I push it into the computer at the desk. Our naked bodies warm each other. He cradles me in his lap and runs his fingers through my hair and kisses my shoulders and neck as I read my declaration of freedom approved by the Galactic Cluster Authority.

My heart drops.

"Does this mean you don't want me?" I ask. Fear closes my throat and I swallow.

"I want you to stay," his lips ghost along my ear and cheek. "Because you want to. Not because you have to."

A smile rises to my lips and I lean my head back on his shoulder, tipping up to a kiss.

I first translate the replicator menu options for my pirate. I write them down on his tablet so he can use it without me. Then, at night, before or after we join, I try to teach him the language. It doesn't interest him. He insists I will always be here to do it for him. I don't deny this.

I start a class for the pirates. First with the intention to teach Fjordooli, but then I realize how many of the crew don't read or write Galactic Common. My class starts with few, but over the cycles it grows. I am proud to be their teacher. They are fast learners. No one gave them a chance before now. I can understand that.

Taren leaves me to my work and I leave him to his. Over time the crew calls me scholar. At first I think it's in jest, but now I sense reverence from them. I love this title. I love my students. I love my new purpose.

I think now, maybe, Parishioner is proud of me.

Many cycles later, I lose track, I am with Setsui in Vabselin Station. It drifts through the inner cluster. Never being in one place for too long. I have not been to many stations, but we have so much money from the replicator, even I have my own to spend on its array of goods. She takes me to the center with shops lit up with neon signs like the ones I longed for in Disca. Taren is somewhere, handling business, and so my friend takes me to see the sights. We eat food.

Drink drinks. Play some street games for prizes. I win a stuffed pesnort for Taren.

We find ourselves in an expensive clothing store. The clerks are mostly human and smile when we enter. The dresses of cascading fine fabrics catch my eye in the window. I touch the pretty things, carrying my stuffed pesnort. Setsui has no interest in the clothes and sits in a chair by the dressing room as I try things on. I lace up a white gown flowing from my hips. The back and front are low cut with lacings. I tie it off and open the door to show my friend.

Varashka stands before me. His pink eyes gleam as they rake down and up over my curves.

"Just for me?" he asks, taking hold of my wrist and yanking me against him.

I search for Setsui and find her on the floor. Her lifeless green eyes stare up at the ceiling with a smoking hole from a fresh gun wound on her forehead. In her hand is her pistol. Hot. Freshly shot. Singeing the plush purple carpet beneath. I heard nothing over the blaring music in the dressing room.

I can't breathe. The store clerks huddle against each other, crying. This can't be real. It must be another nightmare. But his grip is firm and pain in my chest tightens as he drags me to the back service door. His men are with him and more wait for us in the hallway behind the store. I scream and when Varashka throws me over his shoulder I kick and punch. He grunts and swings me down. I land on the ground, on my rump. A companion of his presses a white cloth against my face.

We leave my pesnort behind in the dressing room. We leave my friend on the floor.

6. Taren

I finish business with the exotic pet dealer, another hundred thousand speks in the bank, and check my comm. Setsui is supposed to check in with me every hour. My crew follow as I track her beacon to the shopping district. It's fancy. Just my girl's taste because I know this ain't Set's doing. Outside the store, Galactic Cluster Authority officers cordon off the area.

My heart pounds in my throat.

"No," I say, pushing my way through the gathering crowd. "No. No. No."

My crew trail behind me. The officer plants himself in my path. I stare him down and he steps back. He knows me. They all do. I pass them to the empty store. Two girls cry into each other as an officer attempts an interview. I round past a rack of clothes and see her. My first mate. My friend. She's dead.

Anger fires my heart back into life. Dennon runs to her and checks for vitals. The poor fool loves her. Then I think of my own love. I search the dressing rooms and find a stuffed pesnort left behind with rumpled clothes on the floor. That's all. I close the distance to the crying girls.

The officer stammers and I shoulder her out of the way.

"What happened?" I ask. Trying to keep my cool.

They shake their heads and cry.

"What, happened?" I try again. They blubber and I grab one's silk collar, pulling her face close to mine.

"Tell me."

She swallows, "A b-blue man. Alien. Shot her and took the other."

"They went through the back," her friend points.

I tear through the store and kick open the back door, whipping out my pistol. The alley's empty. No signs. No clues. Nothing. They're long gone.

First thing's first. I return to Setsui and lift her in my arms. Gods she's heavy. I ask Dennon to grab Samiyah's things in the dressing room. Past the officers and crowds I haul Setsui to Whydah. Dennon helps me clear the way and in time I set her down on the infirmary bed. I withdraw the replicator from my hidden jacket pocket and slide it on. I gasp and shake my arm as the cold metal climbs up. Its freezing temperature gets me every time.

I close my hand over Setsui. The replicator vibrates. I know I can clone something alive and something long since dead. But I haven't tried to clone something sentient. A someone.

I shake my other hand at Dennon, "Tablet. Get my tablet."

He returns and I flip through Samiyah's translations to navigate the menu. Our time is limited. I know we need a few of Setsui's cells to be alive. My hand shakes. Samiyah's beautiful writing distracts me from the task, but I figure it out. I've done this enough times to not be shocked by the gaping hole left in my friend's blue skin by the replicator.

Or the warm bright light that follows. But a screaming, wriggling, wet baby in my hands does. I breathe out a held breath and laugh. It worked. I think.

Dennon pulls a towel from a drawer beneath the bed and we swaddle the baby. It's not a bad job considering neither of us handled one before now.

I hope this works. I hope she's intact.

I disengage the replicator and it shrinks back into a plain ring on my finger. I slip it off. Now, on to the next task. Finding my woman.

7. Samiyah

I wake up in a familiar room on Varashka's ship. He sits at his desk, studying me. The viewing window opens to a spiral galaxy in the distance. Its white tendrils flow outward against the black of dark matter. I remain in the dress from the store, tags hanging off of one shoulder. I sit up and tuck my legs beneath me. This can't be real. But it is. My head pounds from the chemical they used to sleep me. My wrists are red from the bindings, which are missing.

Varashka leans forward in his chair, his forearms resting on his legs.

"Oh, my love," his voice is soft. "How long I have looked for you."

My mouth is dry and I can't find words.

My instinct is to tell him he will regret this. He will suffer. For taking me away from Taren, but then again, I am not sure. Taren has his replicator. I translated all of the words on it for him. I may not be worth the trouble to him. As he says, he can find beauty anywhere. Even another Fjordooli scholar. I cannot count on him to get me out of this. He may not reciprocate that impossible feeling I have for him.

I swallow and cross my arms over my chest when I catch Varashka's gaze lingering on the outlining curve of my breasts.

"I did not want to be found," I finally say. I do not understand how my lady hasn't spoken with him yet. "I do not belong to you anymore."

"Oh, that," he stands up and approaches. I slink away until my back bumps against the tapestry hanging above his bed.

"She told me, but it's not true. You have always belonged to me. Always," he sits on the edge of the bed, in arms reach. "Isn't that right?"

I shake my head, "I don't understand."

"You don't remember me," his dark brows furrow. "Do you?"

I study him, "No. I do not."

He sighs and caresses my cheek. I flinch.

"Do you remember Matgha?" he asks.

"What?" Of course I remember Matgha. When I arrived at the ranch, he was my first friend. Even before Parishioner. He was a stock like me. He gave me little gifts. We would sometimes talk together. For hours. Laugh together. I sang for him, danced for him.

"What have you done with him?" I ask.

A laugh wells up from deep within Varashka. Heat flushes my cheeks. He calms himself and leans in.

His breath ghosts along my cheeks as he whispers, "I am he."

"What?" I gasp. Matgha is a child. Bright red. A similar species but, "Impossible."

"Is it?" he brushes a wisp of hair behind my ear. "Do you remember when I asked you to run away with me? You said no. You broke my heart, but it's all right. I forgive you. I know now that you were afraid. You were loyal. Conditioned. Brainwashed. You had to be with your future master. So I have done everything in my power to make sure *I* become your master."

My heart thuds in my chest. I mourned Matgha when he was sold. His loss is what drove me to seek out Parishioner's company. He is why the old man became my friend. But the pain of it faded with time. I moved on, as I had to.

"You were a child," I say.

"So were you."

I shake my head. "This cannot be."

"I'm a Serfin."

I struggle to pull my knowledge of Serfins from memory. They grow fast. They molt their skins at different intervals of their lives. I raise my hand to my mouth, searching for any familiarity. His eyes. They are the same. Something about him that hasn't changed. How did I not notice before? I used to stare into them for hours when we talked. It is him.

"Matgha?" I ask.

He smiles, but shakes his head, "No more. No longer. I am Varashka."

At first, happiness. My friend is alive and well. But is he truly well? No. He is not the same.

"You did this all for me." It is not a question. My heart beats fast and heat flushes my cheeks.

He nods, proud.

"You killed my friend," I ball my hands into fists. "You took me from a happy home."

"Sami—"

"You are a murderer!" I slap him. Immediately, I regret it. He holds his cheek and crimson seeps into the pink of his eyes.

"What happened to you?" I ask with tears spilling down my cheeks. He is alive, but not in the same sense. Matgha is dead. This Varashka has taken his place.

"I killed her. My new master. I killed her in her sleep. That is how it began, but not how it will end."

I flinch from his caress.

"I have done everything for you. With thought of you, and finally I had enough to ensure you would be mine. I'm sorry I was angry with you at first. I was disappointed you didn't know me, but now I understand that wasn't possible."

"Don't you dare put their blood on my hands," I blurt. "You may say you do this all for me for the next hundred cycles, but it is your choice. These are your sins. I want no part of you. Not anymore. You are not my friend. I want to leave."

He scowls.

"We are both changed," I sigh. "This cannot be."

"No," he grips my chin, forcing me to look into his eyes. "I don't care if you are still pure."

"It is not that," I push my hand against his shoulder as he leans in. "No. Matgha don't."

"Don't call me that," his mouth is on mine. Hard. I turn my head and he latches onto my neck and jaw. I'm on my back, he holds me down with his weight. I try so hard to push him off. He is too heavy. Too strong.

"Do you think," he whispers as he sits up to rip the dress from my shoulders. "A baby will catch? Do you think our mating will produce?"

Tears well my eyes and I thrash beneath him. He takes me in his arms and anchors me to his chest, stilling me.

"Shhh," his breath is hot on my hair. "Shhh."

I sob against his chest.

"Please," my voice muffles. This is not like Taren. "Please let me go."

"I will never let you go," his baritone vibrates against my ear. "Never."

He reaches into his pocket and places a capsule between my lips.

"Bite it," his breath ghosts against my ear.

I shake my head. He forces my mouth open, and clamps it shut over the capsule. My teeth break its fragile skin and sweet liquid spills down into my throat. I swallow as he holds my mouth shut. Warmth spreads from my stomach through the veins of my body. I gasp when he releases me. My hands slide between my legs. This isn't fair. I do not want him. When he fondles my bare breasts and his hand slithers beneath the fabric of my dress to slick folds of heat, I moan, involuntarily. I do not want this.

"That's it," he whispers against my cheek. "Give yourself to me."

He takes his time. Removing my dress. Toying with my unwillingly wanton body. I try to crawl away from him, my backside exposed. He yanks on my hips and his mouth finds the slick heat between my legs. I moan. I can't help myself. Tears slide down my cheeks as I gasp and clutch the silk sheets. It feels so good. I spread my legs for him and push against his tongue. Then he replaces it with his girth. There is no pain. Fulfillment. Pleasure. Self loathing. Nerves of hot sensitivity track down my spine like lightning. It's too much. My breasts bounce with the movement of our joining and my hair falls loose from my braid. I lean on my elbows, letting my head fall to the cool sheets. His hands grip my ample hips as he rocks against me.

I drop to my shoulders and cry out against the mattress as my body reacts. My muscles spasm and he moans behind me. I pant, my hips sticking up, attached to him. He stills with a shudder.

I do not want this. This is false.

I try to escape often. To what end I don't know. I cannot leave the ship. I cannot pilot a shuttle or escape pod. But I hope to find some reprieve from my daily task. Once I claw the air vent cover away from the wall and slip inside. I crawl as far as I can, but when I drop out of it, Varashka waits for me with my collar and chain.

We return to his room and he gives me the sweet pill that makes me burn for his touch. We pant and writhe on his bed when the door hisses open. The drug in my veins prevents me from seeking modesty. Varashka welcomes the mostly human crewmember to watch us, reveling in our display. He sets the tray of food down on the desk and does as he's told, but instead of focusing between my legs where our joining is most obvious, he only looks me in the eye. Instead of lust or desire, what I think Varashka wants from him, I read pity.

I hate it. If you pity me, why won't you help me? When my master and I shudder, the man leaves without a word. I think of the one Varashka killed for letting me escape. I know why he won't help. I don't blame him. If I were him, perhaps I wouldn't help me either.

I lose track of the cycles. They blur. Each one he takes me over and over. In many different ways. Always feeding me the capsules. Forcing me to cry out for it. To beg. To humiliate myself beyond repair.

Only once I am foolish enough to refuse it, and the copulation is painful. Disgusting. Worse. So much worse. Now I never refuse them.

This is not what he claims. This is not devotion. Adoration. This is obsession. I am a prize for him to possess. He shows me off in front of his crew. Any he does business with. Sometimes joining with me in front of them if they wish it. Their greedy eyes watch us. Sometimes they ask to join, but my master refuses them. I am given that mercy. But I do not give up. Even though he reinforces every panel so I cannot leave again, I will escape. I will get myself out of this.

Every time I lay in sweat and semen, panting, I close my eyes and wish. And dream. Of Taren. I miss his touch. His smile. I do not cry anymore when I think of him. I hope he is happy. Healthy. I hope his dreams come true. I hope the replicator brings them to him. I mourn Setsui when I can. I get so little time to myself before Varashka demands my body. I fight him when I can. But sometimes I just don't care. Sometimes I give in, too easily. I take the physical pleasure to drown out the mental anguish. I imagine Parishioner and Taren both being disappointed in me, but I get so tired of fighting.

Parishioner used to speak to me of a hell for his God. A place where the sinful burn in agony for eternity. Eternity is frightening all in of itself. I think I may be in a version of this hell. It lasts forever. There is no fire, but burning can have many meanings.

This is my life now. Destiny has caught up to haunt me. This is what I was always meant to be. Not a scholar. Not a partner. Not the light of someone's life, but the fuel to their burning lust. A prize to be kept locked up in a room. We do not go to Varashka's home. Ever. We keep to the stars, moving always in the ship. Always leaving ports and stations and traveling around. We resupply. He occasionally works, but always returns to me. I wish for his death each time he walks out the door. Once I say as much to him, and with a sharp smile he reminds me that he keeps the crew at bay. Without his protection I am at their mercy. It frightens me into silence and I keep my biting words to myself. He doesn't talk to me as he once did. When we were children. He has no use for my mind as Taren does. Did. He does not want to know my likes or dislikes. My hopes. My dreams.

Occasionally he brings a trinket, hoping for me to reward him with a smile, but I do not. Even if I like it, I pretend I don't.

8. Taren

Another message chimes in at my desk. I watch it. My blood boils as Samiyah's head bobs up and down over Varashka's lap. He says nothing. Never does. Doesn't need to. I clench my hands into fists. If I catch him...I *will* catch him. I will get her back. I will drink his blood.

I slam my fist against the wall. My desk screen lowers. I let out a held breath and lean back. I pluck Samiyah's picture off the wall and trace my fingers over it. I took this without her knowing, not long after Sylvester died. This is when I noticed my feelings for her. And when the monster from the deep grabbed her, I couldn't imagine living without her. The translation in her pouch was a second thought. I forgot about it until she was safe and sound on Whydah. How could this happen to me? Me?

Gods I love her.

At first, I'll admit, I just wanted to fuck her like everyone else. She is beautiful. The rumors are true. But it isn't her ass and hips I miss. It's her smile. Her laugh. Her warm touch. When she laughed and cried about the concept of freedom when I first met her, on the ranch, I realized she's a person. She has hopes and dreams. I doubt any of them are to spend her life on her back or knees. And when she cried over Sylvester's dead body...she was in such pain. I can't remember feeling pain like that. I can't remember feeling anything like that, before that moment.

Guilt restricts my chest. I could have done so many things differently. I shouldn't have forced them down there. I should have left the old man alone. Perhaps he would be alive today if I didn't. I shouldn't have lied to her, manipulated her into getting what I wanted. But if Sylvester was here...would we be together? I won't trade anything for my time with her. But we aren't together now, are we? That will change.

I stare at her picture. She is pure. Her emotions. Her spirit. She's smart. She's selfless. How many people put themselves in danger because it's simply asked of them? And...why do I go on like this? I know why I love her. Now I need to find her.

When Sylvester made me promise to keep her safe, to keep her from that asshole, I thought it would be easy. A simple task. That alien shit is nothing to me, and yet here I am. Chasing him. Chasing her. I should have killed him. I should have let him find us and ended it before this began.

I sit up and let the picture flutter to the rumpled bed. I stand and cross over to the radar map to follow moving icons of ships nearby. I will find her. I don't care if I have to comb through every station and ship in the cluster. I will find her. No one hides from me like this. He knows I'm coming for him. I hunt people for a living. For fun. And I can't find this asshole. He must have his hands on the new invisi-light drive.

I should have told her I love her. I should have told her long ago. Now I'm afraid I won't get the chance. No, I can't think like that. I will tell her. Everyday. For the rest of our lives. I withdraw the silver band set with a blue diamond from my pocket. I had Sylvester cremated and condensed into this gem. She can carry him with her forever. I will bond her with this. I hope she likes it.

The door to my cabin hisses open and Setsui prances in. She ages quickly. She's still a child, but she retains her memory. The experience of her previous life mixes with the emotions of her current. A dangerous combination of intelligence and bratty attitude. I laughed for days listening to a toddler swear her vengeance and threat of disembowelment on Varashka.

"Hey!" she smiles and offers me a crayon drawing of her and Samiyah. "Look it what I made."

I laugh and pat her head.

"Good job. That's really going to help find her. Maybe we can post these as flyers so people can tell us where she is."

Setsui glares at me, but I'm busy thinking.

We haven't tried that. Posting a missing person reward. Samiyah helped me make this money. Gods know I can use it to help find her. I snatch her picture from the bed and sit at my desk. Setsui jumps on the bed behind me. I'm used to this by now. What a charming little shit.

I tap into the network of the Galactic Cluster Authority and start a reward based missing person/alien/other file. I scan her picture in. My fingers halt over the keys. Then I type in seven figures. That should be enough. Embarrassing I have to resort to this, but my pride can't keep me from her. I put in my contact information under anonymous. This can hurt my reputation.

Setsui watches and lays her small hand on my shoulder, "Don't worry. We'll find her."

"I know," I say, patting her hand.

In the meantime, I have to continue on living. We make our stops. Sell our exotic animals and rare plants revived by the replicator. I can't spend all of my time looking for her. I tried and the crew gets restless. They like her well enough, some more than that, but the majority think I need to let her go.

Never.

9. Samiyah

We dock at a space station. The viewing window is open and I press to it. Varashka's body weight pushes me against the glass. My breasts flatten on the cold, smooth surface and my hands slide along trying to find purchase that can't be found. I moan, my breath fogging to condensation. He lives in a fantasy that all on the station can see us joining. And it is possible, I suppose, that some can. I squeeze my eyes shut, ready to finish. Crying out he shudders behind me and we pant. He leans his hand on the window and I gasp as he separates us.

His fingers trail over the slick curves of my body.

"Together three-hundred cycles today," he whispers. "Don't worry. Soon we will produce. I will get help. A baby will catch."

He finger combs my hair as I stare at the movement of other ships and shuttles beyond. Their bright lights flash past. Neon signs glitter and run along tracks. I wonder how many others are shut in as me. How many others are stuck on those docking ships? I long to leave this room.

"Won't that make you happy?" he asks, as though he actually cares.

I know he won't listen to what I say, so I say nothing. He likes to pretend I am happy. He likes to pretend this is what I want. I watch his reflection behind me smile.

"I have something for you," he steps away.

I turn, leaning my hot skin against the cool glass. He offers me a parcel and I cock my brow. I pull the ribbon wrapped around it loose and the parchment paper falls. Clothes.

I haven't worn clothes, real clothes, in some time. He gives me flimsy things. Small pieces of cloth one can allude to clothing, but nothing this solid. I can't help myself and snatch them up. A tunic. Pants. Something I can wear to feel like myself again. Something to remind me once I was a scholar. Once I lead the way to ancient relics. Once someone cared about me. That impossible thing I cannot have.

I swallow and Varashka cannot help himself grinning as I tug on the black cotton clothes.

"Does this make you happy?" he asks.

I give him the gift of my gaze.

"Yes," my voice is small.

"I'm going to station," Varashka dresses himself. "Do you need anything?"

He always asks me this, and I never want anything, but today is different.

"Yes," I say. I sit on the bed.

He pauses, then finishes buttoning his pants.

"Anything," he says.

I think, my freedom. But I know this is pointless. Instead, "A pad of paper and a pencil? Not a tablet. Those."

He nods.

He kisses my forehead, as though he actually cares about me, excited.

"Of course, my love. Anything for you."

He leaves, the door hissing shut behind him.

I shower, as I always do, to get the feel and stink of him off of me. Out of me. I relish in my clothes when I slip them back on.

I sigh and stare out the viewing window. Our room always smells like copulation. I tire of it. I glance to the rumpled sheets. The computer screen that faces the bed. He records us joining often. I do not know the purpose, but I suppose it does not matter. I am his to do with as he pleases. I cannot see anything in this room without a reminder of something we have done in a joining. I am never allowed to leave except under lock and key. A delicate collar and chain keep me to him when normally I would run. I have thoughts of running to the dock and letting myself out into the vacuum of space. But there is eternal hope he will tire of me. This is a possibility. My lady always says it is possible and warned me against it, but his interest does not fade.

Movement catches my eye in the viewing window as a ship closes in to dock at the station. My heart leaps in my throat. I recognize it. I will know it anywhere. The Whydah. I jump up to the window and wipe condensation from our joining away. Past the smeared coat I can imagine Taren in the pilot's chair on the bridge, bringing it in. Complaining about dock masters and their rules. I smile. He must be there now. So close. So far.

In foolish vain I beat my hands on the glass and shout for him. I cry for him. Tears in my eyes, I search the room for a means of escape and look back to the ship I know so well. Even my Parishioner could still be there, in one form or another. I pace before the window. I know the door will not open to me. It never does. Only to Varashka or one of his crew. One stands outside right now, guarding me. He will not dare come in without Varashka. He is meant only to keep me in, and others out.

I take a deep breath. Then braid my hair back. I rip a piece of cloth from the bottom of my new pants to tie it off. I search the room. Weapons lay about, but I do not know how to use any. Varashka has no fear of me. I pick up a long wooden pole. He uses it to practice. He comes in with it, sweating and tired sometimes. I think this is a weapon, but it is simple. I think I can just swing it.

I climb up onto the desk with the pole. I know what I must do. Make it sound like I'm trying to escape or hurt myself. This always summons the guard. I cry out and jump to the floor with a thud. The door hisses open and the crewmember searches for me. I hit him with the pole. It cracks against his green face. He cries out and stumbles back. I hit him again and the stick breaks against his stomach. He falls backward. I strike him in the head until his eyes close. He breathes, lying in the doorway, keeping it open. The hall beyond him is empty. I grab his pistol and hold it like I watched Taren do many times.

Taren. I will find you. I must.

I run down the hall with the pistol. I don't know how to shoot it. Or to aim, but I do know to point it at things. The first crewmember I come across, I point it at his face. He reaches for his own weapon, but perhaps it's the desperation in my voice or the look in my eye that freezes him.

"Take me out," I say. My hands shake, my voice does too. But I am serious. I will figure this gun out.

He does as I ask. I recognize him as the crewmember who brings my food.

"The back way. I know there are back ways. Unseen," I say.

He nods. As we walk along he glances over his shoulder, "I will help you."

"I know," I keep the gun trained on his head, not paying attention to where we go.

"I will anyway," he looks ahead. "I pity you, slave girl."

"I do not want your pity. I want your assistance."

He nods and stays silent as we navigate the ship. Every time another crewmember rounds a corner or steps into view, the man is quick to duck us out of the way. In several places I know he can take my gun, overpower me, but he doesn't try. I believe he may be honest. But it is too late. He should have helped me three hundred cycles ago. Where was he then? Surviving, like me, I suppose.

We reach the dock, but there are too many here. I try not to despair. My eyes dart around at all the crew. The man ducks behind a box of cargo with me. A gate tunnel connects the station to the dock. If I can reach the gate, I can get to the station. I don't know if I will find Taren there. He doesn't always go to station, but his crew does.

"I'll distract them," the man snaps me out of my thoughts of the pirate captain.

"What?" I ask. "Will you not get in trouble?"

"I think I'll be okay."

We lock eyes. His are blue, like my Parishioner's. Perhaps this is foolish, but this alone makes me trust him. I nod.

"I will run then."

He snatches the gun from my hands and I gasp. I flatten myself against the box, watching with wide eyes as he flips a switch on the pistol.

"It's useless without the safety off."

He offers it to me, handle first.

I will my heart to climb back down from my throat as I take it.

"Th-thank you."

The man mutters a wish of luck before he sneaks round to another door. He disappears and a moment later appears at another doorway. Far from me. He runs in, panting. Exasperated. The others turn to him.

I sneak from box to box while they ask after his exertion.

"She's gone," he pants. Sweat rolls down his face.

"Who?" another asks.

I am so close. I need them to move, just a little.

"Who do you think?" the helpful man asks. He gestures to the door, "The girl. *The* girl."

They swear and close in on him to ask what he found. He lies. Someone must have helped me. They all draw their guns. And run. Only one remains. An alien woman. She holds a gun and her purple eyes dart around the dark shadows of the cargo bay. I swallow and hold up my gun, aiming it at her.

She gasps and grips her weapon. Though my hands shake as I approach, my gaze does not.

"I only ask you let me pass," I say. She glances at the doorway. More crewmembers are here. Some shout when they see me.

The woman points her gun at me, yet I know she cannot shoot. I run. Fast. My bare feet gain traction on the cold metal surface of the cargo bay. She reaches for me, but I duck out of the way. Then the doors to the dock hiss open and I run down the tunnel connecting the ship to the station. More of Varashka's crew drop their wares and shout. I shut my eyes and point the gun upward. I squeeze the trigger. The laser blasts and bounces around the hall. They scream after me. I don't stop and shoot again.

Samiyah

The second laser penetrates the glass and compromises air pressure. Red lights flash and the doors begin to slowly shut. The gun is hot in my hand and I drop it when I slide through the doors to the station. They lock shut behind me.

There are people everywhere. I push past them. Running down the walkway opening up into a multilevel complex of stores and shops. Loud music. Dancing figures. Beautiful. Neon. Free. In the crowd I cannot hope to find Taren, but I search for anyone who might know me. Anyone from Whydah.

I push and shove, earning glares. There is so much going on. So much activity. I will never find him here. I stop and lean against a metal column lit up with a square panel. My wind catches me and I hold my side. I cannot breathe. Varashka will know. Soon he will return and know I am gone. I cannot go back to that room. I will die if I do.

The panel on the column fades into a new post and I gape. My picture, and in common below it offers a large reward. Anonymous. He's found out already? There's a button to push if you see me and my eyes dart around. No one notices yet and I cower behind the column, keeping my face towards it.

If I cannot find Taren, I must go elsewhere. In this port, like so many others, there are no Galactic Cluster Authority stations. There are none to uphold the law but mercenaries like Varashka. No one cares I am held against my will here. I cannot ask for help.

10. Taren

I sign the tablet the dock master waves in my face. Gods I hate them. Setsui hangs off my arm, excited to look around. I have to remind her she can't go drink in her favorite bar yet. Even here she's too young. She crosses her arms and cocks her brow. I hate teenagers.

I double check the cargo I came here to sell. Then we head into the main station. Lots of decks to navigate. It's a nightmare if you don't know where you're going. I notice Samiyah's picture flash across the public panels every once in a while. It aches in my heart. I'll find her soon.

"Captain," Dennon, from the ship over the comms. "He's here."

I know who, "Where?"

"I don't know, but he's docked. We're scanning the station now, but it's going to take some time."

All business forgotten, my hand itches for my pistol. I will make an example of him, in front of everyone. Maybe kill him with my hands. Definitely not the pistol. That's too quick. I may have put too much thought into this. I also have slow torture in mind, but my love may disapprove of that. I smile, thinking of her frowning and shaking her head at me. Just to see her upset with me is something to look forward to.

Now, the hunt is on.

11. Samiyah

I walk, keeping up movement. The longer I stay in one place, the more likely I can be found. I am not far from the ship.

I do not know all of Varashka's crew, or Taren's. I am not sure who I can trust. My face lights up another screen; this one large, in an eatery. To my relief none of the patrons look up from their meals. My stomach rumbles and I hug myself. I must keep going.

I cannot tell if I walk in circles. All of the beautiful neon signs and dancers and music and restaurants look the same to me. I tire and sit at a table on the main walkway. I need to rest. I lay my face on my arms.

A hand on my head wakes me. I yawn and blink. Varashka sits next to me. I gasp and sit up. I stand and he grips my wrist, yanking me back down to my seat. I shake my head, swallowing.

"How di—"

"You are beautiful, but not very bright. Are you?" his voice is soft as he insults me. He strokes my cheek. "A tracker sewn into the lining of your clothes."

I hang my head, fisting my hands in my hair. It loosens from the braid. Varashka pets me.

"Come with me," he pulls my hands free. "You're not in trouble."

Samiyah

I shake my head and tears spill from my eyes. I can't go back.

"Shh," he caresses my cheek. "I know you're upset. Soon a baby will catch and—"

"No," anger spurns strength from within me. "I want no baby with you. You disgust me."

Red clouds his pink irises. He raises his hand and I shut my eyes, but no pain follows. Instead he clutches my wrist and stands. The patrons around us eat their meals in silence, their eyes resting anywhere but on us.

I yank, his grasp is firm. I wrench and lurch, thrash and command he let me go.

"I will never be good enough for you," rage totters at the edge of his voice. "Tell me you love me."

"Never," I spit.

He jerks me against him and kisses me. The mercenaries meant to keep the peace in this station look the other way. This isn't their business. I do not pay them.

Varashka gets in my face, his eyes crimson.

"Tell me you love me," he shakes my shoulders.

I ball my hands into fists and swipe my knee up into his groin. He releases me and I stagger away. I slip past his crew, running through the crowd. There is no rhyme or reason to my direction. Just, get away. I can't go back. I can't. I don't care if I run to my death. I must be free. I hear them behind me, colliding with patrons and tables and chairs in their haste. Varashka shouts after me. I jump over benches, tables, chairs. Anything in my way I clear, but my side hurts. I can't keep this up. My legs tremble with each duck, each dodge, each turn. I stumble into the table of an eatery along the main thoroughfare. I lean against it. I can't breathe. My lungs are on fire.

Varashka claws my shoulder and spins me around to face him. I pant. He slaps me. The sting resonates and I cup my hand over my cheek. I grit my teeth and ball my fist to strike him, but he catches it.

"You know," he hooks the delicate collar around my neck, panting. "You might have gotten hurt. Someone who doesn't care for you as I do might have taken you from me. You will find a way to love me. We will produce. You will love our child." He hooks the chain to the ring of my collar. "We were always meant to be."

I shake my head. Anger, hate, sadness all boil within me and I scream his name. *His* name. The only one that matters. Just once. It's hopeless. Futile. I know, but I cannot help it. I cry for Taren.

Varashka laughs as he tugs on my chain.

Taren slides out from a crowded store behind my captor. He whips out his pistol and shoots it into the air. The crowd screams and scatters. The mercenaries raise their guns at Taren, but only a moment. As if they know him, they lower their weapons and step back. Leaving him to his business.

We turn, Varashka uses the chaos, dragging me behind him. We slip into the running crowd.

"Taren!" My heart sings at the sight of him. So close. I plant my feet, forcing Varashka to drag me. I take hold of the chain and pull, but he is too strong. We lurch forward. People and aliens and others duck into stores around us. The crowd thins.

Now there is a clear way from Taren to us. His mouth is firm, grim. His black eyes focus in anger.

"Varashka!" he hollers behind us.

We do not stop. We do not even turn back. We head to the ship. I glance over my shoulder. Taren follows.

"Samiyah!" he shoots his pistol again. This time it hits a column next to us. He misses on purpose. His aim is perfect.

My captor halts and withdraws a pistol. He fires back. I grab his bicep to throw off his aim and he throws me to the floor. Lasers fly. I crawl away and Varashka catches my ankle. He drags me back, my cotton clothes sliding along the metal polished floor.

"Stay here!" a laser flies past his face. He shouts and cups his cheek. When he lowers his hand, a singed black line mars it.

Taren draws close, shooting his gun, walking, slow. Steady. Confident. Varashka's faulty aim shoots lasers past him. They both fire until the guns click, out of charge. Varashka grabs my chain and I choke as he drags me along the floor. I cannot help myself. I reach out for Taren. He runs and jumps over a table separating us and tackles Varashka to the ground. He releases my chain. Taren strikes my captor. Again. And again.

Varashka slides out from beneath him and topples the pirate with a kick. Taren falls and rolls into a recovery, on his feet. They circle each other. Taren shrugs off his jacket and withdraws his hunting knife from his belt. Varashka rolls his shoulders and unsheathes his own. Both their crew stay back.

A girl runs past them to me and kneels down. She tugs me out of the way. Her skin is blue, her hair pink. She is familiar. Her eyes are green like home planet.

"Samiyah?" she cups my face and forces me to look away from the match. She shows no concern for the fight close to us.

In the corner of my eye Taren and Varashka swipe at each other. Taren catches Varashka's wrist and hits it against the column with all his strength. I turn from the girl. We watch in silence, holding each other.

The blue mercenary drops his knife and pulls another. He slices through the air, cutting through Taren's leather skin tight tunic. Blood runs from the gash, but the pirate isn't fazed. He jabs at Varashka and makes contact with his rib cage. My captor cries out and doubles over.

Taren balls his fist and strikes Varashka's jaw. He flies back and lands with a crack on the floor.

"This is what happens!" the man in black shouts over the music and advertisements to the onlookers peering from behind tables and shop windows. To the mercenaries who watch with their guns slack in their grip.

"This is what happens when you take from me," he stands over Varashka. He stares down the mercenary's crew. They don't move. He leans over Varashka, "All of your training and you are shit. All of your scare tactics and big talk. You are filth. So tough, but you hide from me. For how long? How many cycles? You took what is mine. *Mine.*" He beats his fist against his chest and points down to Varashka's bleeding face.

"Mercy," my captor begs for the one thing he did not give me. "I have only taken what belongs to me."

"She was never yours," Taren's voice softens. Quiet. Dangerous.

My heart beats back to life. This is for me. He means me. I am his. And I think he is mine. I grasp the girl's hands.

"And he falls, like a sheep to the lion," Taren steps on Varashka's chest, leaning on it. The mercenary gasps and coughs beneath his weight. My captor grabs the pirate's ankle in a weak grip. Taren places his knife against Varashka's throat, ready to kill like the men of ancient times.

My eyes dart between them.

"Taren," I swallow.

His black eyes flicker to me.

"Mercy is stronger than death," I quote Parishioner. A small part of me, very small, mourns the boy I knew. The boy I cared for. "Do not add him to your sins."

His brows furrow, Varashka panting beneath him.

"This *is* mercy," he says, driving the knife across Varashka's blue scaly skin. Rose colored blood spills from his throat.

I know I should be sad to see a life end before me, but I am not. I can think only of the past three hundred cycles. How many times he pushed into me. How many times I cried in the night. How many times I wished for freedom, even if it meant death. As the light of life leaves his pale pink eyes I grieve for the boy I once knew. Not the man who kept me chained to his bed. I am both sad, and happy.

Taren steps off. He wipes his knife on his leg, sheathes it. He picks up his spent pistol and holsters it. He pants and turns.

"Come," he says.

I launch myself upwards to him and he takes me in his arms. I cry. So much. So hard. So long. Relief washes over me. We stand, time stills. He is warm. Gentle, firm. Mine. He pulls away, taking my face in his hands. I can hardly see him past my tears. I tilt my chin up to him.

"I love you," he says.

I jump into his arms and squeeze him with my limbs. His breath is hot in my hair. My lips ghost along his neck.

"I love you," I whisper.

There it is. That impossible thing I was always told I can never have.

We are in his room. Our room. My favorite place. The stuffed pesnort left behind in the dressing room sits on the dresser. My clothes that were with it are folded next to it. My picture hangs by the viewing window. He missed me. He loves me, he tells me everyday, almost as much as I love him.

We join many times. He does not care Varashka was in me. He does not care the things I did to survive. He loves me as I am. He tells me always. Again. And again. Everyday.

I lay on my side under the sheets as he leans over the edge of the bed. He finds what he seeks and rolls over to face me. He brushes loose hair behind my ear and smiles, bringing our lips together. He holds up a silver band with a blue diamond. I tilt my head, staring at it.

"I can't bring him back," his dark gaze lingers on the gem. "But I had him made into this."

My eyes water. My Parishioner. The diamond is the hue of his eyes. His kind eyes. Memories flood my vision as Taren slips it over my finger.

"He brought us together," his voice is a whisper. "But I will keep us so."

Our fingers interlace. We are bonded. In blood. In lust. In life. In love.

I am free.

THE END

Samiyah

L.R. Hicks

About The Author

L.R. lives in Washington amongst the trees and mountains, enjoying hiking, camping, and writing when the mood suits.

L.R. Hicks

More From LeeLoo Publishing!

"Absolutely hilarious!" "Brilliant. Fun read!"
"Actually laughed out loud!"

marq truong

Brick Wilson: For Hire by Marq Truong

Brick Wilson's adventure takes the reader crashing through universes, galaxies, circuits and alternate realities where anything can and does happen. On his search for the lost Pesnort, Brick is continually challenged by dangers real and imagined as he skillfully avoids the Ultimate Galactic Headquarters Tax Authority, dodges the increasingly menacing plots for his demise by arch nemesis Terd Murchison, and is continually stalked and mocked by the color Red. Can he save the Pesnort, the Universe and himself with a psychotic android in tow?

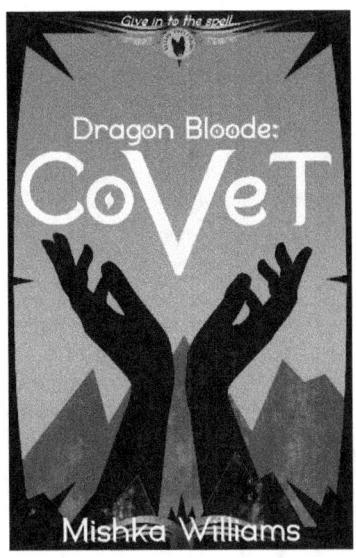

Dragon Bloode: Covet by Mishka Williams

Dragons.
Once a mighty race of winged gods, they're reduced to three. No longer do they resemble the scaled flying marvels of their ancestry, but the humans who interbred with their forefathers.
The Bloode is thin and dying.

Mishka Williams's dark fantasy debut is nothing short of spellbinding. Dive into a realm rich with magic, Dragons, and lust. Set against a gothic backdrop in the world Alperin, Williams takes you to the Draak Empire. Rife with division between the Emperor and his Dragon generals, the empire faces enemies on all fronts.
From the Fae, the Elves, and from within.

L.R. Hicks